Lily found her eyes drifting to his mouth, felt the vibration of that memory—the carnal craving, the need that had been as instinctual and primal as taking a breath.

She had felt sure she would die if he stopped.

She lifted a mental screen and pushed the memories behind it before they overwhelmed her.

'People try for years to get pregnant,' she said, thinking of her twin. 'I didn't think anything would happen the first time—which was stupid.'

Benedict's dark brows lifted. 'You *think*?' There was a hard, ironic gleam in his eyes. 'A child...' He dragged a hand through his hair, a dazed expression on his face as he turned his scrutiny on her. 'So I have a child and you didn't think to mention it to me? I wasn't a stranger...'

'You didn't owe me anything. It was my decision to have Emily—my responsibility.'

'So you made a unilateral decision?' He struggled to keep a lid on his anger.

She lifted her chin. 'Yes, and I'd do the same again.'

HER NINE MONTH CONFESSION

BY
KIM LAWRENCE

First published in Great Britain 2015
by Mills & Boon, an imprint of Harlequin (UK) Limited,
Eton House, 18-24 Paradise Road, Richmond, Surrey, TW9 1SR

© 2015 Kim Lawrence

ISBN: 978-0-263-25871-4

Kim Lawrence lives on a farm in Anglesey with her university lecturer husband, assorted pets who arrived as strays and never left, and sometimes one or both of her boomerang sons. When she's not writing she loves to be outdoors gardening, or walking on one of the beaches for which the island is famous—along with being the place where Prince William and Catherine made their first home!

Books by Kim Lawrence

Mills & Boon Modern Romance

One Night with Morelli
Captivated by Her Innocence
The Petrelli Heir
Santiago's Command
Stranded, Seduced...Pregnant
Unworldly Secretary, Untamed Greek
Under the Spaniard's Lock and Key
The Sheikh's Impatient Virgin

Seven Sexy Sins

The Sins of Sebastian Rey-Defoe

Royal & Ruthless

The Heartbreaker Prince

One Night With Consequences

A Secret Until Now

At His Service

Maid for Montero

Protecting His Legacy

Gianni's Pride

**Visit the Author Profile page at
millsandboon.co.uk for more titles.**

For Shirley.
She was the best mum—a brave and lovely lady.

PROLOGUE

London. Three years earlier.

IT WAS SIX A.M. when Lily woke, thanks to her internal alarm clock—an inconvenient genetic quirk that always woke her at this hour. She knew she wouldn't be able to snuggle down and have another half-hour under the duvet, but for a few moments she resisted pushing her way through the thin layer that separated sleep from full wakefulness.

On the plus side she was never late and it was amazing what you could achieve in that quiet hour or so before the rest of the world, or at least her loud neighbour in the adjoining flat, woke.

She silenced the tedious inner voice that insisted on seeing the bright side of everything with a scowl and pushed the heavy swathe of tangled curls from her face. Lying there with one arm curved above her head, she focused on her justified resentment of people who could roll over and fall back to sleep. Normal people who overslept, even her own twin, Lara, who, it was no exaggeration to say, could sleep through an earthquake. But no, not her, every morning it was the same old…same old…

Only it wasn't.

A fresh furrow appeared between her delicately delineated brows as a remaining sleepy corner of her mind told her actually something *was* different, but what?

Had she actually overslept?

Eyes closed, she reached out for her phone on the bedside table. Patting her hand flat, she hit a couple of unfamiliar objects before she found it. Opening one eye, she glanced at the screen and read the predictable and unsociable hour. She clutched the phone to her chest—*naked* chest! Was that relevant? she wondered as she hitched the sheet up over her shoulders. No, the *something* different was not the time or her naked state.

So what was it?

She looked around. This was not her room.

The belated recognition hit her as she struggled to focus. Her entire body felt as though she'd just run a marathon—not that she ever had or in all probability ever would. But last night...*last night*!

Her green eyes snapped wide open as the memory of the night before hit her like a bolt of lightning. At least that explained the aches in places she hadn't known she had.

She pressed a hand to her left breast where her heart was trying to batter its way through her ribcage. The rush of blood in her ears was a deafening roar as she turned her head slowly...very, *very* slowly. What if she'd been dreaming? She gritted her teeth, prepared for an anticlimax that never came.

A fractured sigh left her parted lips... It was real, not a dream; *he* wasn't a dream.

She blinked, bringing the face on the pillow next to hers into focus. A stab of sizzling longing lanced through Lily's body as she greedily absorbed the details of his symmetrical features, committing each plane and angle to memory. Not that she would ever forget him or last night!

He had a face that inspired a second glance and inevitably a third. The sleeping man's chiselled bone structure was dramatic, a broad intelligent forehead, high carved cheekbones, square chin with a sexy cleft, thick darkly defined brows, an aquiline nose and wide, expressive mouth. If pushed to select an individual feature that set him apart, Lily decided it would have been his eyes.

Beneath heavy lids and framed by lashes that were as dark as his hair and crazily long, his eyes were the deepest, most electrifying blue she had ever seen.

Looking at his sleeping face now, there was something different about him. It took her a few seconds to work out that the subtle difference was something that *wasn't* there. It was an absence of the restless energy that hung about him like an invisible force field when he was awake.

It would have been an overstatement to say it made him look vulnerable, but it did make him look younger. Even with the dusting of stubble in the hollows of his cheeks and across his jaw there were enough reminders of his younger self to make Lily's thoughts slip back. Memories that were now tinged with a rose-tinted nostalgia that had been absent that first time she'd seen him.

She'd *known* about him, of course. The estate, where her father was the head gardener, and the village had been buzzing with gossip about Benedict, the boy born with the silver spoon, the boy doted on by his proud grandfather. While everyone else had got excited about the fact that he had just moved into the *big* house, Lily had nursed a quiet and growing resentment.

Warren Court, one of the most important houses still in private hands in the country, was just five hundred yards from the estate cottage where Lily lived. She had known, even then, that in all other ways it was a planet, a whole *universe*, away. She had been totally prepared—actually determined—to dislike the rich boy.

And then her dad had died and she'd forgotten about Benedict, not even seeing him standing beside his grandfather at the funeral. She had thought no one had seen her slip away when she'd escaped from the churchyard and headed for the pond where her dad had skipped stones from one side to the other.

Something he'd never do any more.

She'd picked up a big stone, weighing it in her hand before launching it into the air. Her heart had felt like the stone as she'd watched it sink, then another and another until her arm had ached and her face had been wet with the tears she'd ignored. But she hadn't been able to ignore the voice or the crunch of leaves as someone had come to stand behind her.

'No, not like that, you need a flat one and it's all in the wrist action. See…' She'd watched the stone skip lightly across the water.

'I can't do it.'

'Yes, you can. It's easy.'

'I can't!' Fists clenched, she had rounded angrily on him, tilting her head because he was so tall. She'd vented her grief and frustration at the intruder, screaming, 'My dad is dead and I hate you!'

That was when she'd seen his eyes. So blue, so filled

with sympathy as he'd nodded and said simply, 'I know, it stinks.' Then he'd handed her another stone and she could still remember how it had felt smooth and cold on her hand. 'Try this one,' he'd said.

By the time they'd left, she had made a stone skip three times and she had decided she was in love.

It had been inevitable really. Lily had craved romance and the boy who was almost a man had seemed like the amalgam of all the heroes in the novels she devoured. Not only had he lived in a castle, but to her youthful self he had seemed like the embodiment of a dark and brooding hero. Mature—he was five years older than her—sporty, sophisticated. Lily had woven an intricate web of wildly unrealistic fantasies around him. Fantasies she'd dreamed would come true. Until the night of the ball...

She had been waiting for weeks for the annual estate workers' Christmas party, hosted by Benedict's grandfather in the massive Elizabethan hall of Warren Court, where her mother was now the housekeeper. She knew that Benedict, who had graduated from Oxford that summer and was doing something important in the City, according to his grandfather, would be there.

Lily had spent hours getting ready. Persuaded Lara, who had much better fashion sense and many more clothes thanks to the tips she got at the hotel where she waitressed on Saturdays, to lend her a dress. Then finally Benedict had arrived and the first thing she'd noticed was how different he'd looked, remote somehow in his sleek dark suit. Before she'd had time to absorb all the details, she'd seen that he wasn't alone.

'I am *so-o-o* bored, darling.' The tall designer-dressed blonde, who had spent the night sneering, hadn't even bothered lowering her upper-crust voice with its tortured vowels as she'd drawled, 'When can we leave? You didn't tell me the place would be full of the local yokels.'

Followed by Lara never missing an opportunity to tease Lily about her ill-disguised crush. 'Drooling, Lil? So *not* a good look, sweetie. If you want him, go get him.'

Lily had finally snapped. 'I don't want him. I don't even *like* him! He's boring and totally up himself!' she'd declared before she'd turned and seen Benedict standing behind her.

Since that embarrassing moment she hadn't seen him or thought about him, not for years. Obviously his high profile meant that she saw his name sometimes, though not often—the financial pages were not really her thing and she didn't have a clue what an investment tycoon was.

What she hadn't expected was to bump into him coming out of a bookshop.

She didn't believe in fate but...well, what else explained it? She had walked out of the door and at the exact same moment he had been walking by. Blinded by a strand of hair whipped across her face by a gust of wind, she had walked into him. Not any of the other people walking by—*Benedict*.

Coming out of her reverie, she clenched her hands tight as she fought the compulsion to touch his cheek. His deeply tanned skin was dusted with stubble that was the same ebony shade as the thick hair he wore cropped short. He was sleeping so peacefully and, though sleep had ironed out the lines of strain that ran from his nose to his mouth, the dark shadows under his eyes remained. Tired looked sexy on him, she decided as her fascinated gaze lingered on the shadow cast by his long spiky eyelashes against sharp cheekbones.

She released the breath trapped in her tight chest in a slow sibilant sigh. He was *beautiful*. Yesterday she'd had to bite her tongue to stop herself saying it, then she hadn't. She'd said it over and over, she'd said it in between kisses and while she'd kissed her way across his chest.

They were lovers.

Her first... She hugged the knowledge to herself, a dreamy expression drifting into her eyes as her thoughts slid back to yesterday and the moment that had changed her life. It had changed her; she felt like a different person...

'Lily!'

Benedict had always been one of the few people who *never* mistook her for her twin.

He handed her the book that she'd dropped and fatally his tanned fingers brushed hers. No teenage sexual fantasy—so safe because it had never been going to happen—had prepared her for the nerve-stripping effect.

The electric sizzle shook her so badly she barely remembered her name as slowly they both rose to their feet, the book they both still grasped acting as a connection they seemed reluctant to break.

It was a passer-by bumping into them that made them break apart, the book falling again to the floor.

The spell broken, they both laughed.

This time she let him pick it up. Staring at the top

of his dark head, she gave herself a mental shake and put some defensive tension into her spine. She saw him raise a brow when he looked at the title and this time when he handed it to her she made sure to avoid contact. This triggered a quizzical look that she didn't react to beyond the flush she was incapable of controlling.

'You always were a bookworm,' he said, smiling. 'I remember the time I caught you in Grandfather's library, you hid his first-edition Dickens under your jumper.'

'You remember that?' She stopped in her tracks, her amazement giving way to horror. 'It was a *first* edition?'

'Don't look so worried—the old man didn't mind.'

'He knew?'

The lines that fanned out from the corners of his eyes deepened as her astonishment drew a laugh from his throat. 'That you used the place as an unofficial lending library? Well, he did, he doesn't miss much... so...' He lowered his gaze from her flushed face, turning his wrist and with a flick of a white cuff revealing his paper-thin watch.

Lily watched with a smile she really hoped said *I'm in a hurry too.*

The next time you are in danger of believing in magical connections, Lily Gray, she told herself, *or a sexual awareness too strong to deny, remember this moment.*

'I was going for a coffee...' He stopped, his remarkable eyes filled with warmth and other things that made her stomach flip as he gave a twisted, rueful smile and admitted huskily, 'No, I wasn't, but I am now.' Head tilted a little to one side, he smiled into her face. 'If you'd like...?'

Her knees just stopped short of buckling. They were shaking. She released a carefully controlled sigh, her emotions a mingling of excitement and fear as she thought, if a smile could do this much to her what would a touch do…a kiss…?

Getting ahead of yourself here, Lily. He's offering you a cappuccino, not a night of wild, head-banging sex! It was just coffee, she reasoned.

'Yes.' *Too keen, Lily.* She gave a smile. 'I'm not meeting Sam until half four.'

His dark brows twitched into a line above his masterful nose. 'Is Sam your boyfriend?'

'A friend,' she said. And it wasn't a lie: Samantha Jane was a friend, the first one she'd made at the drama college. Sam wouldn't mind if she was late; Sam would approve. She often lectured Lily on her love life, or lack of it.

'You have to stop being so picky,' Sam had told her. 'Look at me—I've lost count of the number of frogs I've kissed but when my prince comes along I'll recognise the difference, and actually frogs can be fun.'

An hour later Lily and Benedict were still sitting in a cubicle in a small coffee shop and she couldn't remember what they'd talked about. But she had made him laugh, and he had made her feel smart and sexy. He thought she was funny so she was. After the first five minutes she had relaxed and lowered her guard as their conversation moved from literature, to politics, to her favourite ice cream, to her drama school course and the great opportunity that had recently fallen in her lap. It was only later she'd realised that he'd hardly told her a thing about himself, but then it was, oh, so easy to be wise with hindsight.

'So I'm going to see you on the big screen?' Elbows on the table, he'd leant forward, his interest seeming genuine and unfeigned. He had ignored all the women who had eyed him up, not even seeming to notice them. It seemed he only had eyes for her and Lily was flattered. If she'd been a cat, she'd have purred.

'A small part.'

'I'm not sure actresses are meant to be self-deprecating.'

'I'm not, just factual. It's a small part.'

'But the TV drama, that's the lead?'

'I've been really lucky.'

'You could do with a few lessons in self-publicity.'

She looked at him through her lashes and asked huskily, 'Are you offering?'

His slow smile made her insides melt and her heart race even faster.

Over her third cup of coffee, looking into his electric-blue eyes, Lily made the dizzying discovery that it was potentially addictive having a man look at you with undisguised desire. Especially when the man in question had, for a large part of your life, represented the perfect ideal and you'd spent your life measuring other men against him—inevitably they had fallen short.

Could that be why she'd still not had a single serious relationship?

The possibility drifted into her head and then was gone because he had caught her hand and, holding it between his thumb and forefinger, was massaging the pad of her palm. The light arabesques sent deep tremors through her body. What she was feeling bore no resemblance to any teenage crush. It bore no resemblance to anything she had felt or imagined feeling.

She didn't even know she'd closed her eyes until he spoke in his deep husky voice.

'I have a room.'

She didn't say anything; she couldn't.

Her voice sounded throaty and deep, unfamiliar to her own ears, when she finally managed a response: 'Yes.'

If she'd known what she was saying *yes* to she wouldn't have waited even that long. Last night had been more than Lily had ever dreamed!

Her body still thrummed with the sensual aftermath of their lovemaking and her heart felt full. And there was more to come, much more, there were days and nights and... She felt her heart flutter as she thought of a future with Benedict in it, beside her in her bed. Last night was the start of something...it *had* to be.

Not romanticising, she told the voice of caution in her head. The sex had been incredible but it had gone beyond the physical; nothing *that* special could be transitory. She had no name for it, but it had been real.

'What are you waiting for, Lily?'

Lily had never had an answer for Sam's exasperated lectures about lowering her expectations and being realistic.

As she directed her searching, hungry gaze at his face a series of sensual images superimposed themselves over his sleeping features. The accompanying taste and textures were so real that the effort of separating herself from them brought a fine sheen of perspiration to Lily's skin.

She shivered even though she was close enough to feel the warmth of his body. She had an answer to Sam's question now—Benedict was the man she had been waiting for.

Did he realise that he'd been her first? Last night the memory of Lara's experience had made her hold back. The man her twin had fallen for had said virgins were not his style—*a deal breaker*, she remembered Lara saying, while she outlined her solution to the problem.

Did other men feel that way…?

Did Benedict?

Would it be a *deal breaker*…? Could she take the risk?

Did not telling him constitute lying?

In the end the moment had passed, as had the fear her inexperience might be a problem. But she still didn't know if he'd realised.

She would ask him, she decided, fighting the strong compulsion to wake him, her lips curved in a contemplative smile. Lily lay down with a sigh and, in an effort to distract herself, began to scroll idly through her emails before moving on to read the latest theatre gossip. She discovered, as her fingers idly flicked through the website, that the play she'd seen the previous week had been nominated for an Olivier award and the fans of a soap were demanding they reinstate a recently axed daytime favourite. A celebrity couple were splitting but staying good friends and a—

Her finger froze as she stared at the screen. The images there screamed silently back at her until she felt as though her skull would explode with the building pressure, the anger aimed as much at herself as him.

'No!' she whispered, but though the words and images blurred through the tears in her eyes they remained there, visible evidence of her wilful stupidity!

The piece was written in a gushy style that included quotes from friends of a newly engaged couple. There were several photos of the bride-to-be, the shiny rock on her finger and the groom…the groom…looking handsome on a ski slope, snow on his eyelashes…looking elegant and aloof at a red-carpet event…looking dynamic and sombre at an economic conference.

Her chest lifted in a tremulous sigh as she started breathing again and turned her head.

'Nobody is surprised,' she'd read.

Well, they were wrong; she'd been. Self-disgust left a rancid, metallic aftertaste in her mouth as she asked herself, *Why are you surprised? You saw what you wanted in him, not what was there. He's a man, and you were an easy lay.*

Anger and devastating hurt clawed at Lily's throat as she struggled to swallow a sob. Hands clenched, her nails gouging deep into the soft skin of her palms, she turned her hard, glittering stare on his sleeping face.

At sixteen she'd seen through him; she'd had more sense then than she did at twenty-two! Even if he had assumed that she was perfectly all right with one-night stands, he was engaged, *newly* engaged, for God's sake!

On the brink of waking him, confronting him, Lily pulled back, breathing hard as she struggled to regain some control. Would venting her feelings of outrage, would the satisfaction of confronting him, be worth exposing her own humiliation? It would be tantamount to admitting she was a naïve idiot who believed in soul mates and true love.

Anything, she decided, was better than that!

Shaking from head to toe, she pushed back the covers, freezing like a creature caught in the headlights when he groaned. She waited, heart hammering, until his breathing had settled into a deep regular pattern again before standing up.

Naked, she moved around the room, shooting wary glances at the sleeping figure as she gathered her clothes. She dressed in the bathroom, not daring to put on the light, and slipped like a thief into the early morning. It felt furtive and sordid, but then, she reflected grimly, it was.

It wasn't until she was on the tube that she realised she had lost one of her earrings.

It wasn't the only thing she had lost. But what Lily didn't know then was that she had also gained something…

CHAPTER ONE

FOR THE FIRST two days of her holiday Lily had put on a sundress over her bikini, applied some clear gloss to her lips and a light smudge of eye shadow before walking, sandals in hand, along the white sandy beach. She'd joined the other guests in the dining room, a structure with a roof but no walls. In the evening, guests could eat and listen to music provided by a talented in-house pianist, while watching the sun go down over the ocean as they sipped exotic-looking, but lethal, cocktails.

Pretty much idyllic with one small but significant negative: Lily had no one to share the experience with. This was not a problem for her, just other people, it seemed. So this morning, she'd decided to have her meals on the patio of her beach-front bungalow.

'Just ring through if you'd like lunch here too, miss.'

Lily smiled at the maid, Mathilde, who had come to collect her breakfast things. 'I thought I might explore a little, walk into town maybe, so afternoon tea would be better and I'll have my dinner here.'

'Alone?' The maid looked almost as disapproving as her mother would have.

Lily nodded firmly.

To say you couldn't move without falling over honeymooners was a *slight* exaggeration, but the adult-only luxury resort was, unsurprisingly, geared towards loved-up couples. The only other singleton Lily had encountered was a chatty middle-aged travel writer. While it was interesting to know that the island had once belonged to Denmark before they sold it to America, another lecture over dinner tonight did not appeal.

And besides, these days being alone was something of a treat. Until you were a mother, she mused, picking up her towel and setting off along the white sand in the opposite direction to the maid, you could never quite grasp how much your life changed.

Not that she'd change it, she thought, her expression softening into a warm smile as she thought of her daughter. Motherhood might not have been something she'd planned, but Lily could not imagine her life any other way now. She missed Emmy so desperately, it actually felt as though she had a body part missing. But there was a guilty pleasure in spending half an hour on her nails and a couple of hours reading without interruptions.

Still, a new laptop—the third prize in the magazine competition—would have been a more practical option.

'You can't pass up a holiday in a tropical paradise!' Her mother had been outraged by the suggestion.

'But Emmy...'

'You think I can't look after my granddaughter for a week?'

'Of course you can. But I couldn't possibly let you...'

Lily felt guilty enough as it was that she relied on her parent so much. Her mother had been incredibly supportive all the way through her difficult pregnancy and then a real sanity saver during those early sleep-deprived months. Lily would never have been able to take on her part-time job if her mum hadn't been there ready and cheerfully willing to look after Emmy on those two mornings she worked at the local college.

'What would I do on this island of sea and sand?'

'That you have to ask shows how much you need this holiday. When was the last time you had a half-hour to call your own, Lily? When did you last spend some time socially with anyone your own age? You need to let your hair down. You might even meet someone…?'

Lily gave an exasperated sigh. She knew exactly where this was going. 'I know you want to see me married off, Mum, but—'

'I want to see you happy, Lily. I want to see both my girls happy.'

Lily knew what 'happy' meant to her mum, who was fond of saying, 'There's someone out there for everyone—a soul mate. I found mine,' she added. 'There was never and never will be any other man for me but your father.'

Lily had always struggled to reconcile the misty-eyed romanticism with her childhood memories of angry raised voices, slamming doors and tears. Lily never voiced her thoughts, she felt disloyal for even thinking them, though she sometimes wondered if her mum really felt that way or if it was her way of dealing with being widowed so young. Had she been telling the stories for so long she believed them…?

'I am happy, Mum.' Why did no one believe her?

And even if she had been looking for romance, she had no time for it. Juggling her part-time job in the college drama department and the unpaid hours she put in at the hospice—where her mother fundraised so tirelessly—with caring for her two-year-old daughter left no time for anything except falling into bed exhausted at the end of the day.

Lily considered her life rich and fulfilling. Occasionally she thought *what if...?* But those thoughts were swiftly quashed. She still had ambitions; they just weren't the same ones she'd had as a final-year drama student. Back then she'd had several small parts in TV dramas under her belt and the lead role in a new costume drama to walk into when she graduated—not bad for the *invisible* twin.

But her life had changed unexpectedly and she didn't resent it. Now she wanted more than anything to be a role model for her daughter. Although she'd been an OK actress, she had discovered by accident she was a *better* than OK teacher. As soon as Emmy was in school she had plans to get the qualifications to enable her to lecture and not just be an assistant. She might never see her own name in lights, but she might be responsible for some other shy, awkward kid—as she'd been—discovering the liberation of becoming someone else on stage.

Lily's thoughts were not on her future career as she wandered down the deserted beach, her feet sinking into the sand. She was replaying the conversation she'd had via the computer link with her daughter the previous evening. Well, *conversation* might be overstating it. Emmy had fallen asleep after five minutes on her grandmother's knee saying loudly that she wanted a dog, a *wiggy* dog.

'She means waggy, I think,' Elizabeth had translated, stroking her granddaughter's curly head. 'She grabbed Robert's poor old Lab by the tail and wouldn't let go.'

Lily's eyes misted as the longing to hold her daughter, smell her hair, brought an emotional lump to her throat.

Dropping her towel on the sand, she stared out to sea, the ache in her chest a mixture of pride and loneliness as she waded out into the warm, clear water.

Returning the painting had been a theatrical stunt. The big reveal had gone down like a lead balloon, but in his defence Ben had tried everything else. Nothing had worked. His grandfather had refused then, as he did now, to give an inch. He still refused to concede that selling off the odd heirloom or parcel of land was not a fiscally sound form of long-term financial planning.

This morning the argument had not gone on long before his grandfather had given his *never darken my door again* speech and Ben, knowing that if he stayed he'd say something he'd regret, had accepted the invite.

Striding through the corridors of the old house, he'd predictably felt his anger fade, leaving frustration and the realisation that he needed a change of tactics. Governments and financial institutions listened to his analyses, they valued his opinion, but he just had to accept that his grandfather didn't even think of him as an adult, let alone someone qualified to offer advice.

He'd paused, responding to a text from his PA reminding him he had a meeting in Paris in two hours, when he heard the sound. Glancing through the deep stone-mullioned window at the helicopter he'd arrived in, which was sitting on the south lawn, Ben was tempted to pretend he hadn't heard it. Then he heard it again—the sound of a child crying.

Curious, he slid his phone back into his pocket and followed the sound of the cries. The search led him to the kitchen, a room that, like the plumbing at Warren Court, would have made a Victorian feel right at home.

The door to the vast room was open, and as he stepped inside the source of the noise, a child held by his grandfather's harassed-looking housekeeper, Elizabeth Gray, let out an ear-piercing screech, made even louder by the room's tremendous acoustics.

'Wow, that's quite a set of lungs.' And quite a head of hair. The wild red curls on the toddler's head opened a memory he'd have preferred to stay locked inside the file marked *move on.*

And he had moved on; it was ancient history.

'Benedict!'

Would Elizabeth's smile have been so warm and welcoming had she known he'd slept with one of her daughters? The lazy speculation vanished as she advanced towards him holding the screaming child. Horror slid into the vacuum it left.

'Your grandfather didn't tell me you were coming...'

'He didn't know.' Ben prided himself on the ability to extricate himself from uncomfortable situations, but for once his ingenuity failed him.

'Are you staying for...? Never mind—hold her, will you?'

It was not a suggestion or a request, it was a plea, which he hadn't responded to when he had found his arms filled with crying toddler. A new experience for him... He stood rigid, holding the wriggling, screaming child the same way he would an unexploded bomb—at arm's length! He'd have felt more comfortable with a bomb; they were more predictable.

Ben had nothing against children, and he understood why people felt the urge to procreate, he just wondered why some did. People like his mother, who had never made any pretence of being maternal. His mother, who had done her level best to forget that she'd had a child after she'd given birth and had done so pretty successfully. She had never made any bones about what came first—her career. And as she'd pointed out, not having a mother coddling him had made him self-reliant.

He recognised similar character traits—some might call them faults—in himself. He was ambitious, ruthlessly focused on his work. Ben had no illusions about his character. Bottom line, he was selfish. That combined with razor-sharp instincts made him successful in his chosen career.

He didn't need those instincts to tell him he'd have been a terrible parent. It was pretty obvious. Being a good parent required sacrifice and compromise, which he was simply not capable of. His decision not to have children was yet another bone of contention between him and his grandfather, who was fixated on the idea of the family name living on.

'Is she ill?' He struggled to hide his unease and eyed the child warily. She might be attractive, but right now, with her crumpled, tear-stained face as red as her hair, she wasn't.

'She bumped her head, slipped chasing the cat. Now let's have a look…it's not deep,' Elizabeth said, brushing a mass of auburn curls from the squawking kid's head. 'But it simply won't stop bleeding and Emmy doesn't like the sight of blood. But she's a brave girl, aren't you, my darling?' she crooned.

The brave girl gave another ear-splitting bawl. Was it normal for a kid to be that loud? Ben, who had been his parents' only *mistake*, wasn't sure.

'I didn't know Lara had a child,' he said, struggling to make himself heard above the din. 'Is she visiting, or have they moved back from the States?' he asked, pretending a polite interest he didn't feel. Though he'd felt mild surprise when the news of the wedding had reached his ears six months after the event.

Lara Gray was the last person he would have imagined marrying young, she'd been a bit of a wild child, but then what did he know? Her sister had always seemed like the last sort of person who'd spend the night with a man and leave before he woke.

But she had.

To wake and find the pillow beside him empty should have been a relief. Yet finding her gone, leaving nothing but the elusive scent of her perfume, scratches on his shoulders and a pearl earring, he'd been furious. While recognising his response as irrational and disproportionate, Ben had struggled to shrug it off. Even now, three years later, the sight of a red curl could flip his mood.

He didn't like being used, and he'd always hated bad manners.

Sure, Ben, you're getting worked up after nearly three years over bad manners...what did you want from her, a thank-you note?

Ben's ego was not fragile and there had been occasions in his life when he would have liked to fast-forward past the morning-after scene. Yet when he had reached across, anticipating contact with warm womanly skin, and found nothing but a cold indent his anger had almost, but not completely, masked that initial gut reaction...*loss.*

It was no use pretending otherwise—the timing had

been bad. He'd known it but he'd still done it. He'd known that his personal life, in the immediate future, was going to be subjected to public scrutiny. His on-off engagement when it came out was going to sell papers, but if it had got out that he'd fallen straight into another relationship, or at least into another bed…was it fair to expose Lily to that sort of smutty tabloid speculation?

You had to laugh at the irony—not that he had. But then what man wouldn't feel a little raw if he'd woken up and found that the woman who had awoken dormant chivalrous instincts—and who just happened to be the best sex he'd ever had—had walked out? But then life was a learning curve and he'd moved on.

He'd rationalised the event. Lily had been what he'd needed, when he'd needed it. He'd just been surprised really—she'd always seemed so…*sweet*. Well, good for her. Clearly she had her mind firmly focused on her career and sex was strictly recreational. He'd met any number of women with that pragmatic attitude; he'd dated more than a few.

'Lara?' Elizabeth, blowing a strand of blonde hair from her eyes, looked up, appearing surprised by the comment. '*Lara* doesn't have children. This is Lily's little girl.'

'Lily is married?' Ben, who had never been one to wrap up unpalatable truths in pretty packaging, found himself not analysing too deeply his powerful gut response to this news.

'No, she isn't married. Lily is a single parent. I'm very proud of her,' she added defensively, explaining, 'She moved back to the village. She works part-time at the college and I help out when I can.'

Ben struggled to take on board all the information and the surprisingly strong emotions it shook loose.

So no big acting career, no glamorous red carpets, no name in lights, just... He looked at the child, who had stopped crying. Tears trembled on the ends of her sooty lashes as she returned his look with one of deep suspicion through eyes that were a deep blue.

Cobalt blue.

He stiffened as somewhere in the back of his mind the seeds of a crazy suspicion sent out tentative roots.

'That must be a struggle.' His sympathy elicited a nod.

'Oh, I love helping... Just hold still a moment for Granny. Emmy is a total sweetheart but Lily...'

'M...Mummy...' Ben watched the child's lower lip tremble ominously before she gave another sniff, her small rounded chin jutting pugnaciously as she yelled, 'Want Mummy now!'

'A child who knows her own mind.'

Elizabeth laughed. 'She certainly does, not at all like Lily. She was always the easy one. Lara, now that was another story. Mummy will be home soon, darling, five more sleeps. Hard to explain time to children.' Elizabeth gave a grunt as she successfully taped down a sticking plaster to the child's forehead. 'All done.' She clapped her hands.

Ben watched as the kid followed suit, clapping her chubby little hands. His brain was working but his thoughts kept coming up against a big brick wall. He couldn't see past it because there was nothing to see. He was making the classic mistake of trying to make the facts fit a theory. In this case a totally crazy theory!

The tension that had climbed into his shoulders eased a notch as he recognised the trap he had *almost* fallen into. His mouth twisted into an ironic self-mocking smile. A lot of people in this world had blue eyes; presumably the kid's father had been one of them.

A moment later his smile vanished. As the child continued to squirm in his arms he caught a glimpse of something. A nerve beside his mouth jumped. Blue eyes were not unique, but how many people beside his own mother had that distinctive birthmark? he asked himself, fighting the urge to lift the child's hair to examine the pigmented crescent closer.

'M…M…Mama…' The kid caught hold of his tie and shoved the silk into her mouth.

Who did she call dada?

'Don't do that, Emmy, you'll choke.' Her grandmother prised the soggy cloth from her mouth and directed an apologetic smile at him. A look of concern crossed her face. 'Sorry about… Are you all right?'

Ben inhaled, dredging deep into his inner resources to force his features into something that passed for a smile. 'I had words with my grandfather.' It suddenly seemed a long time ago.

The explanation was accepted by Elizabeth, who held out her arms for the child, the furrow between her brows deepening as he made no move to react.

The question he'd refused to acknowledge slid into his head. Was *the* child…*his* child? *His* daughter?

This was surreal…

It was impossible!

His eyes slid to the baby in his arms and she looked back at him, solemn and serious, then with a grin as she grabbed his soggy tie again.

'Mine!'

Ben felt something break loose inside him and swallowed, reluctant to put a name to the uncomfortable emotion that tightened like a band across his chest.

'No, Emmy! Sorry, Ben...'

This time Ben reacted to the extended arms. As he handed the child over he breathed in the scent of her hair and felt the smooth softness of her cheek. He swallowed. It simply wasn't possible.

Of course it was and he knew it.

Elizabeth took a moment to disentangle the determined chubby hands from the tie, ignoring the shrill yell of frustration when she succeeded.

'Your grandfather misses you, you know.'

Ben shook his head to clear the loud static buzz in his brain. 'He hides it well.'

This was one of life's crossroad moments, when choices changed lives...*his* life...a life he liked the way it was...the life he had chosen. The inner struggle didn't last long, though the resentment of finding himself in this position deepened.

Knowing for sure he had fathered a child was not news he would welcome, but it was preferable to *not* knowing, to live with that question mark.

His shoulders squared with decision as he masked his feelings behind a casual smile.

'So you're babysitting?' Losing the battle to maintain objectivity, he struggled to keep the disapproval he felt out of his voice. He never had understood why people had kids if they couldn't wait to farm them out.

'Actually I have her all week, don't I, darling?' Elizabeth, her expression doting, tucked a shiny curl behind Emmy's ear as the child's head dropped on her shoulder. 'Lily won a prize in a competition,' she explained. 'A week's holiday in the sun.'

His jaw clenched. So motherhood hadn't cramped Lily's style.

'She was going to refuse it.'

Sure she was, Ben thought, hiding his disbelief behind an interested smile.

'I all but had to tie her up to get her to the airport, but it's just what she needs, a bit of sun. She's basically put her whole life on hold, but that's never healthy. I keep telling her, she has to have a life outside of Emmy. But does she listen?'

As Elizabeth chuntered on the image of Lily in a bikini set up a string of images that Ben, despising his lack of control, breathed his way through. He came out the other side feeling resentful and furious at his lack of self-control. Even if this wasn't his kid, he had nothing but contempt for a parent who put their own selfish needs ahead of their child.

'That's an unusual birthmark she...?' He watched for any sign of reaction to his question on the housekeeper's face. Either she was the world's best actress or didn't know either.

'Emmy... Emily Rose.' Her grandmother brushed aside a hank of burnished hair from the child's forehead and touched the small mark near her right temple. 'It looks like the moon, doesn't it?'

Jumping to conclusions in his business was often the difference between success and failure. Sure, gut instinct came into it, but you had to gather data, sift through the evidence, calculate the probabilities before you made a call.

Ben never jumped to conclusions, and now was not

a good time to start. In his experience the best way to kill crazy ideas was throw facts at them.

Clutching at straws, Ben?

Ignoring the inner ironic voice, he asked casually, 'How old is she?'

'Two. She was actually due on the twins' birthday but Lily took a tumble and she came a month early.'

'My mother has a birthmark similar to that one, or she did.' His mother had had it removed while they were doing her first facelift.

'How is your mother?' Elizabeth asked politely.

Ben, who knew the question was inspired by good manners not genuine interest, shrugged. 'I've no idea.' Then, acting on an impulse that he had no control over, he touched a shiny curl before drawing his hand back as though burnt. 'Her hair is just like her mother's.'

And her eyes were just like his. But it wasn't just her eyes: the angle of her childish jaw, the birthmark... In contrast to his slow, measured words, Ben's brain was firmly on fast-forward now. If ever there was a moment to retain the clear objectivity he was famed for, this was it.

Objectivity!

What was the point in objectivity when the truth was staring him in the face? He took a deep breath, his shoulders straightening. Unless someone offered him concrete proof to the contrary, this was his child.

Elizabeth nodded, gave a nostalgic smile and sighed. 'I used to love brushing the girls' hair when they were little. They grow up so fast.'

'It's very...' He paused, the muscles in his tanned throat working as he pushed away the intrusive image

KIM LAWRENCE   35

of curly red strands brushing his chest and belly. The
memory darkened his eyes to midnight blue.

'It's glorious,' continued the fond grandmother. 'It's
from my husband's side,' she confided. 'They have a lot
of redheads, Irish skin and hair. They always burned
in the sun. Not that this little one will have the same
problem,' she said, touching the child's rosily golden
cheek.

Though he felt as though he were bleeding control
through every pore he somehow managed to sound casual enough not to make alarm bells ring as he scanned
the toddler's face and commented casually, 'She's inherited her father's colouring?'

He watched the older woman's expression grow shuttered.

'I don't know. Lily doesn't talk about him.' Her eyes
lowered, hiding her expression as she transferred the
weight of the now-sleeping child from one shoulder to
the other.

I bet she doesn't, he thought grimly. But she would.
When she got back, he'd be waiting.

Why wait?

'Your room, should I...? Jane is around somewhere?'

'I'm not staying, but I'd love a cup of coffee before
I head off.'

He lingered another half-hour and, over a coffee, ex-
tracted the information he needed. A firm believer in
choosing your own battle ground and the advantage of
surprise, Ben saw no reason to wait around while Lily
sunned herself on some tropical beach.

He wanted to see her face when he turned up. He
wanted to hear the truth from her own lips, even if it
was nearly three damned years too late!

Pushing away the image of those lips parting as his mouth crashed down on them, he strode purposefully from the building.

It wasn't until an hour later that he realised why the island paradise sounded familiar.

'So I'll cancel everything for the next, what…three days?' Another person might have sounded stressed, but his PA was her usual serenely unflappable self. Considering he'd contacted her on his way to the airport and told her to free up his calendar.

'Better make it four.'

'All right, four. Will you be staying at the house or shall I book you in somewhere?'

'House?' The question produced a frowning response.

'Have you changed your mind about putting it on the market?'

It finally clicked. She was talking about the property he'd inherited last year from his great-uncle.

'For now. I'll check it out, see if it's worth staying there.'

The flight took for ever. When they finally landed at the private airstrip he arranged for his bag to be dropped at the house, while he headed straight for the hotel that Elizabeth Gray had described as a paradise.

And a prerequisite of paradise was temptation.

Ben lifted a hand to shade his eyes from the sun. He was jet-lagged. No, actually, he'd been jet-lagged when he arrived at Warren Court twelve hours ago. Now walking in totally inappropriate handmade leather shoes along the deserted white sand beach still wearing the same suit, he had gone way beyond mere jet lag.

He was operating on a combination of adrenaline and anger. The hours that had passed since his discovery had not reduced the latter, but the delay had worn his patience to a single-cell thickness.

With his eyes still on the horizon, he dropped down into a crouch and balanced on his heels, examining the sand for the light indents he had followed from her beach bungalow. A redhead was not so difficult to track down, especially when generous tips were involved. A muscle tightened in his chiselled jaw as his efforts were rewarded. The footprints were still there, but they were now heading out to the water.

Straightening up, he altered course, heading towards the towel that lay in a crumpled heap a few feet away. As he picked it up his nostrils flared at the faint but distinctive scent of rose impregnating the soft fabric. He gave a snort of self-disgust as his libido gave a hefty kick.

He still remembered that scent; he remembered everything.

Ignoring the sizzling slither of heat that licked along his nerve endings, Ben muttered under his breath and clenched the fabric in his hands. He levelled his steely gaze at the head of the figure far out in the water. *Too* far given the luridly painted warning signs along the beach that informed of currents behind the reef.

If this day had carried a convenient warning sign he might have stayed in bed. Ben's entire body clenched in anticipation as the figure in the water began to swim towards the shore.

Behind her the water appeared clear azure blending almost seamlessly into the sky. Ahead of her it was turquoise and clear as crystal. The warmth was totally seductive and though she had only intended to stay out for a few minutes she had quickly lost track of time. She was enjoying swimming lazily, though kept in mind the maid's story of the tourist who, after a boozy dinner, had ignored the warning signs or probably not seen them and tragically drowned because he'd ventured past the protective reef.

One of the things she had noticed about motherhood was it made a person very aware of their own mortality and a lot more risk averse. Not that she'd ever been a massive risk taker—well, only once!

Seeing the shore through a watery haze and pretty much spent, Lily paused and, holding her chin up, felt for the sandy bottom, acknowledging the toe contact with a sigh of relief. She bounced along for a few feet, spitting out water before she could place her feet flat on the sand. With the water at shoulder level she walked her way down to waist level, aware as she did so that she wasn't alone. There was a figure on the beach.

She assumed it was one of her fellow guests. This stretch of beach, though not private but because of its remote inaccessibility, was used almost exclusively by the guests at the beach resort. Lily lifted one hand in greeting while she pushed her wet hair back from her face with the other and blinked away the water from her eyelashes.

Then her vision cleared.

For a moment shock wiped her mind as she refused to accept what she was seeing. Her heart thudding with adrenaline-fuelled speed, she closed her eyes, wiped away the moisture with her hand and opened them again.

He was still there, the man in the incongruous dark suit, tall, dark and terrifying familiar. He returned her stare with incredible eyes, the colour rare but not unique—she saw that colour every day.

The last time she'd looked into those eyes she had melted. She didn't melt now, she froze. Every muscle and nerve fibre went into shock. Her brain shut down, a protective response to a situation where she had no other defences to fall back on.

CHAPTER TWO

FOR SOME REASON her baby's father was standing there looking taller and more imposing than she remembered. He was wearing a medium grey tailored suit, white shirt open at the neck—the only concession to the setting. The bespoke tailoring was almost as inappropriate as the tight ache low in her pelvis. Yet somehow he made her feel as if she were the one dressed inappropriately or at least inadequately.

Screamingly self-conscious of every inch of exposed skin, Lily called on all her rusty acting skills and lifted her chin acknowledging his presence with a tiny lift of her hand and an expression of *small world* surprise. Only it wasn't, it was a massive world and he was here. Hard to believe that meant anything good. Pushing through the moment of panic, she forced herself to leave the shallows; the sense of impending doom remained.

Counselling herself sternly not to assume the worst, she took a tiny grain of comfort from the fact that Emmy was safely at home. She wished she were there too as her eyes made an unscheduled covetous sweep up the long, lean length of him. It was pretty hard to pretend to be composed when your stomach felt as if you'd just stepped off a cliff.

But it was sand, not air, beneath her feet and she made herself walk towards him. Lily was so focused on controlling herself and taking that next step that she got within a few feet of Ben before registering the clenched rigidity of his stance. Anger—it radiated off him in waves, and it was all aimed at her. Anger was actually too mild a word for the volcanic aura of antagonism he was vibrating. He pinned her with a stare that was as hard and unforgiving as tempered steel.

Hampered by guilt, fear, a racing heart and a skin-crawling self-consciousness, Lily pushed away the image of her daughter's face and struggled to return the glare with some degree of composure. Beneath her carefully schooled expression her brain was firing off scenarios to explain his presence, all carefully avoiding the most obvious.

He knew!

Fighting the increasingly urgent compulsion to swim back out to sea, she straightened her shoulders and speared her hands into her long drenched hair before shaking it back from her face. Unable to maintain contact with the accusing blue glare for more than a second, she cleared her throat and broke the tense, explosive silence.

'Hello.' She discovered her voice sounded weirdly normal.

Hello...?

She didn't even have the grace to look guilty, she just looked... The muscles in his brown throat worked as he dragged his wandering gaze up the slim length of her sinuous pale curves. The fury he could barely contain mingled with a large dollop of desire. He couldn't deny his reaction when his body still thrummed with the testosterone-fuelled heat that had immobilised him with lust as she'd emerged from the waves like some mythical goddess.

But, in his defence, Lily Gray was the sort of woman who could stop traffic wearing a bin sack. And right now she was wearing very little at all. His eyes made another unscheduled dip. The black bikini consisted of a few triangles of cloth tied together with tiny metallic loops, three in total, one rested between her glorious breasts, the others low on each hip bone. The colour emphasised the creamy, opalescent pallor of her glistening skin. It was every bit as incredible as he remembered it, he thought, hungrily devouring the details. Her body might be lusher than it had been three years ago—in a very good way—but he would still be able to span her waist with his hands.

He looked at them and now realised he still had hold of her towel. The muscles around his jaw tightened as he felt a fresh blast of scalding self-disgust at his lack of control over his emotions. He thrust the towel at her with a grunt.

'Thank you.' Under the cover of a stiff automatic smile, her swirling thoughts raced as she wrapped the soft fabric sarong-wise across her breasts and waited, with a sense of fatalism that approached a Zen-like calm, for him to speak.

When he didn't, she flung a rope of wet hair over her shoulders. She was amazed that her hands were still steady, despite the fact that under the calm, pulses of fear continued to pound through her body and her knees felt ready to give way.

She was living her worst nightmare. If the ground had opened up at her feet, she would have gladly jumped into the black hole.

No obliging hole appeared, so she met his hostile stare with as much composure as she could summon.

'This is a surprise. So what are you doing here?'

'Have a guess?' he ground back, tearing his eyes from the small trickle of sea water running down the curve of her pale, creamy shoulder.

'I was never very good at guessing games,' she blurted, her voice a low driven undertone almost drowned by the low hiss of waves breaking on the shore. 'If you have something to say...?' The tense silence stretched. 'Well, if you'll excuse me I'm late for my massage.' She made to move past him but he blocked her path. The sheer menace of his physical presence would have made her pause if his next words hadn't frozen her to the spot.

'Oh, well, when you can fit me into your *schedule*, I thought we might have a conversation. One like—oh, I don't know... How about: *Ben, it totally slipped my mind, but I had your baby a few years back...*?'

She closed her eyes and thought, *Oh, hell...* Well, maybe now was as good a time as any to get this over with. Sucking in a short, tense breath, every muscle in her body taut, she turned and looked him in the face and nodded.

'Sorry.' Then because it crossed her mind he might think she was sorry she'd had Emmy she tacked on hastily, 'That you found out about it in the way—' She stopped. She didn't know how he'd found out, but she supposed the significant bit was it hadn't been from her. 'This way.'

He clenched his jaw and ground out grimly, 'So you're not even going to deny it?'

A bit late now. 'I'm not a good liar.'

His lip curled. 'Oh, I think you're a *very* good liar.'

'I didn't lie, I just decided not to—'

'Burden me with the truth?'

She winced at the acid sarcasm and began to resent his occupation of the moral high ground as she jerked her eyes up to meet his intense blue glare.

'Or were you just not sure who the father was?'

The insult, because there was no doubt he intended it as such, drew a wobbly little laugh from her aching throat. She clamped her teeth over it and lifted her chin. It was an irony she had no intention of sharing with him. She could at least retain that much pride. Having him know she'd thought their one-night stand was the start of something special would have been too cringingly humiliating; she'd prefer he think she was some sort of bed-hopping tart.

'Oh, there was never any doubt about that,' she said quietly.

'Because I'm curious,' he said, his control straining at the leash. 'Did you *ever* intend to tell me?'

'I thought about it.' Lily didn't register the hissing sound her admission wrenched from his clenched teeth. Her eyes glazed as her thoughts drifted backwards. After the initial shock had worn off she had thought about little else. The tipping point had been the article his ex had written. It had seemed like fate that she'd picked it up in the waiting room before her first appointment with the midwife.

It turned out Ben had only been engaged for five minutes before he'd got cold feet and dumped the poor woman. Commitment phobic, the gorgeous ex-model had explained, but the real breaking point, she had confided, had been his refusal to have a family.

You had to admire the woman. She'd have been perfectly justified, in Lily's opinion, if she'd chosen to stick the knife in. But instead she'd displayed a really healthy attitude focusing on the future, her career change and plugging her new cookery book that was to hit the shelves soon.

That had sealed the deal for Lily. She'd known then that she couldn't tell him.

'But I knew how you'd react,' she continued.

He arched a sardonic brow and ground his teeth in reaction to this claim of psychic abilities. 'And how is that?'

Lily studied his face, her heart clenched in her chest. Even mad, he was beautiful. She spread her hands in an expressive gesture. 'Pretty much like this.'

Before she had become pregnant Lily had never asked herself if she wanted to be a mother. Unlike Ben, who it turned out had decided never to be a father. A man who broke off an engagement because having children was a deal breaker was not going to be happy to learn he was about to be a dad by a one-night stand.

'So how did you find out?'

'How did I find out?' He shook his head and looked at her as though she were insane. 'I *saw* her, I *saw* me...' he ground out, shaking his dark head in an incredulous motion from side to side. 'Your mother doesn't know?'

She swallowed, thinking of all the occasions when she had been tempted to confide in someone, *wishing* she could.

'Not Mum, not... You can relax, I didn't tell any-one.' Not even her twin actually. *Especially* not her married twin, who was desperate to get pregnant and not having any luck. Having always been able to con-fide in Lara, Lily found it hard to deal with this new reality. She just hoped that the wall that had built up between them would be removed when Lara finally got pregnant.

'Relax!'

Lily could feel the anger rolling off him in waves. She struggled to show she was not intimidated by it, but it was not easy when it was buffeting her like a storm-force wind. She bit the inside of her cheek to stop her-self physically retreating from his anger, focusing on the metallic taste of blood on her tongue.

'No one else needs to know, nothing needs to change,' she assured him earnestly.

Lily could hear his white teeth grind as he closed his eyes and muttered under his breath. He opened them again and she staggered from the contemptuous blast of his deep blue eyes. 'It already has changed.'

She opened her mouth to contradict him and her glance connected with his relentless stare. Lily was the first to look away.

'How the hell is it possible for your mother—for *everyone*—not to see?'

'I don't know,' she admitted. On this one point they were on the same page. 'It's always seemed obvious to me but no one else seemed to notice. So I thought why—'

'Bother?' He cut across her, his voice a furious growl. *'I am a father!'*

'Biologically.' She lowered her lashes to hide the hurt

and sadness that surfaced when she thought of her little girl, who deserved a father who loved her.

Ben flicked her a look of incredulous scorn and lashed back accusingly, 'You don't think a child needs a father?'

Lily almost laughed, but she felt suddenly like crying. 'It depends on the father.' Better her baby had no father, than one who didn't want her.

Lily knew that her own dad had loved her and her twin, but the argument she had overheard the night before he'd died still haunted her. Looking back with adult eyes, she was able to see it for what it had been— a couple with money problems fighting, saying things they didn't mean. But she still remembered how it had felt when her dad had yelled, *Why do you think we've got no money? You're the one who wanted to keep them.*

Lily shook herself free from her silent depressing reverie. At her sides her hands clenched. *No.* She would protect her baby from ever feeling unwanted.

Just the baby?

Hadn't there been the smallest hint of self-preservation in her decision? Having Ben in her life, a constant reminder of her romantic self-delusion, would not have been easy to deal with.

It would have been agony. Just looking at him, she thought it *was*! She was no longer naïve enough to call it love, but the primal reaction she had to him was not something she could control, even if it was just sex.

The quiet rebuttal caused Ben to draw a breath. His smouldering gaze dropped, his lashes brushing the slashing angle of his cheek that hid the flicker of uncertainty in his blue eyes. He wondered, *wasn't she right?*

His own father had been marginally more involved in his life than his mother, not because of any genuine fatherly feelings but only in the sense that he'd cared more about appearances.

Would he be any better?

Self-doubt was not something that kept Ben awake at night. He'd made his share of bad decisions. The secret was being prepared to take responsibility and live with the consequences of those flawed decisions, even life-changing ones.

But this hadn't been his decision.

But it had happened, *so deal with it, Ben!*

'So you decided to take me out of the equation.' Just saying it out loud made his anger spike hotly. That it was an equation he had never wanted to be part of did not lessen his sense of outrage or his determination to do the right thing, for his daughter.

'I didn't think of it quite in those terms, but yes… if you like.'

'And you were only thinking of Emily Rose?'

The underlying mockery in his voice brought her rounded chin up. 'It's my job.'

'And you decided that her life would be better without me in it…?'

Not fooled by his light conversational tone, Lily didn't react. She stood there watching him warily, determined not to let him see that his comment had slipped under her defences.

'What about what *she* wants?'

She angled an uneasy look up at his lean face. 'What do you mean?'

'A child shouldn't grow up feeling unloved or un-wanted.'

'She isn't!' Lily shot back, furious at the suggestion.

'You were happy to let her think her father doesn't love or want her. Did you pause when you were making your unilateral decision to think how *she* might feel a few years down the line thinking that her father had rejected her? How that might affect her emotional development, her future relationships? You're willing to deprive her of what you had...what *you* took for granted... Well, I'm not.'

The statement had more impact because Ben clearly wasn't canvassing for the sympathy vote; he was simply stating a fact. Despite this, or maybe because of it, Lily felt her own tender heart soften. A child herself at the time, it had never occurred to her to wonder why Ben had come to live with his grandfather. That he had been unwanted had not even crossed her mind.

'I'm going to make damned sure that *my* daughter isn't going to grow up thinking she's to blame. She'll have what every kid deserves. What I—'

Didn't have, Lily completed silently as he paused for breath. She trawled her memory trying to think of a single occasion when she had seen Ben's parents at Warren Court after Ben had moved in. She came up blank.

'I'm sorry that you were an unhappy child, but—'

He pinned her with a cold blue stare. 'This isn't about me. It's about what is best for *our* child. You may feel it's some sort of badge of honour to struggle financially but—'

'I don't!' she protested, smothering a dangerous wave of empathy along with the image of a sad, lonely little

boy. Ben was not a little boy any more; he was a powerful man. A very angry, powerful man. And he was
angry at her. 'You never wanted children…'

'And you *wanted* to put your career on hold just as
it was taking off?'

'That's not the point!'

His brows lifted as his lips tugged into a triumphant
smile. 'Exactly. Even if I was the total rat you think I
am, even if I had been given the option and chose not to
be part of her life, I have a financial obligation at least.'

'This isn't about money!'

'No, it's about a hell of a lot more,' he growled. 'More
than your selfish pride. So save me the poor and proud
of it speech. My daughter is going to have all the advantages I can give her, so get used to it.'

'You think you can just appear out of nowhere and
take control?' She managed to project scorn, but below
the surface there was a strong steady pulse of fear feed-
ing into her bloodstream.

He shrugged and gave a wolfish grin that left his
blue eyes hard and cold. 'Now you come to mention
it, yes.'

Despite the sun beating down she shivered, suddenly
icily cold. She recalled a recent article in which a rival
had called Ben Warrender a *'wolf in designer clothes,
who wouldn't even get a crease in his suit while he casually destroyed your life for profit'*.

Even allowing for a certain degree of bias, there was
no doubt that in the business world Ben was a preda-
tor. And not the sort of person who was accustomed to
hearing people say no in his personal life either.

'You've had a shock,' she said, attempting to sound

placatory. 'You won't mean any of this when you calm down—'

'I know I've had a bloody shock! I don't need you to tell me!' His eyes narrowed as he added with bitter emphasis, 'Except you didn't, did you?'

'I want nothing from you,' she babbled, close to blind panic now. 'We need nothing from you. What was the point in telling you? There was nothing to discuss then or now.'

Ben's jaw clenched. 'Did you hear nothing I just said?'

Her eyes flashed as she felt a sudden energising spurt of anger. He was acting as though it had been an easy choice, acting as if the thought of bringing up a child alone had not terrified her!

'Yes, and the only thing you're right about is that this is about Emmy and what is best for her. And a father who doesn't want her isn't.' She'd reminded herself of this inescapable fact every time she'd found herself retreating into a fantasy happy-ever-after world where Ben would see his baby and be smitten; he would fall in love with her. Miracles happened—they'd made a baby and that was the greatest miracle of all.

'It is not a question of *wanting*. It has happened.'

Lily found the awful grim tone of acceptance in his voice was a million times worse than his anger. 'I didn't do it on my own!' she quivered back.

He reacted defensively to the guilt that felt like a stomach punch. 'I took precautions!'

'Well, they didn't work!'

Something in her expression made him pause. He'd been so caught up with his own feelings…for the first time he found himself wondering how an unplanned

pregnancy had made her feel. Had she been scared...
angry...? Had she hated him?

Was keeping him in the dark her way of punish-
ing him?

Why the hell was he feeling guilty? Maybe being irrational was contagious...

'Well, you've got me there.' His drawled response
drew a wary look of suspicion from her gold-shot green
eyes.

'I don't want to have you...'

He raised a sardonic brow.

'Anywhere?' She closed her eyes and thought, *Shut
up, Lily.* 'I need to get indoors.' Half turning, she
dropped her voice to an indistinctive mumble. 'The
sun... I burn.' Her eyes lifted and connected with his.
The searing heat from his blue stare was several thou-
sand degrees more scorching than the morning sun
beating down on her bare shoulders.

'You think I'll be an awful father.' He hid his very
real fear that this was the case under a casual shrug.
'Maybe you're right, but the fact is we're going to find
out.'

'But you don't want—'

Roughened with impatience, his deep voice drowned
out the rest of her protest. 'Don't tell me what I want
and don't make this a fight, Lily, because you'll lose.
Save the mutual recriminations. The situation exists so
let's deal with it and move on.'

Where? 'I can't!' she yelled wildly and began to run
along the beach, the tears streaming down her face.

By the time she reached the bungalow Lily was out
of breath. Chest heaving, she sat down on the bottom
step covered by the shade of the canopy and waited.

There was nowhere to run.

A few moments later she heard his approach. She carried on staring at the sand until his feet appeared, the handmade leather dusted with sand. Her gaze travelled upwards until she reached his face. Despite everything her pulse leapt. She pressed her lips together to stop them quivering and held his gaze.

'That was childish, sorry.'

Ben tried to hold on to his anger but the glimmer of tears in her big green eyes made it slip away. She looked so vulnerable that he had to fight down the urge to offer her words of comfort. Instead he dropped down onto the wooden step beside her and waited. None of this was turning out the way he'd imagined.

Lily stiffened as the painted wood creaked slightly. Though she stared straight ahead, in the periphery of her vision she was aware of him brushing sand from his trousers before resting his hands on his thighs.

'I know we need to talk,' she finally conceded, turning her head and angling a pleading look at his face. 'But can it wait until later?'

There was no receptive softening in his face to her appeal. 'I think I've waited long enough, don't you? I haven't been there for my kid because I didn't know she existed.' He dealt her a grim, twisted smile. 'What's your excuse?'

Her chin lifted as her cheeks heated with a combination of lust and guilt. She surged to her feet bristling with hostility as she stared down at him. 'What do you mean by that?' she tossed back in a low, throbbing voice.

He shrugged. 'I'm not the one who dumped her baby on her mother to cavort half naked on a tropical beach.'

And she's not the one who is struggling to focus past half-naked.

'I didn't *dump*… I've never spent a night away from Emmy before…' A suspicious furrow appeared between her feathery brows. 'Are you trying to make me out to be a bad mother? Are you trying to take Emmy away from me?' Breathing hard, she pushed away, a paralysing stab of visceral fear hitting her. If he wanted a battle she would give him one, but she would never give him Emmy.

'Don't go paranoid on me.' Ben roughed out his annoyance, giving way to admiration as he got to his feet and stood looking down at her.

Her determination to regard him as a threat continued to be maddening and frustrating, but her tigress-like reaction to a perceived threat to her child…he couldn't help but admire that.

'You love her,' he conceded with a shrug.

'Of course I do! I'm her mother!'

Ben found himself almost envying the fact that she took this as a given. What would Lily make of a mother who had no problem with her baby calling his nanny Mummy? A situation that his own mother had been quite happy with until the nanny had been caught in bed with her husband.

'I can see that. And because you love her I'm assuming you agree that she needs stability.'

'She has stability.'

'So what happens when in the future—' A future that would include men… His jaw clenched as he imagined a procession of faceless lovers drifting in and out of his daughter's life—*and Lily's bed*.

'When what?'

'My child—'

Lily felt something inside her snap. '*Your* child. Where were you when *your* child had colic or when she...?' Closing her eyes for the count of ten, she dug deep for calm, which she claimed after huffing out several breaths.

'Sorry, that wasn't fair, but neither were you.' She flashed him a look of simmering reproach through her long curling lashes. 'I may not be a perfect mother.' It was a steep learning curve. 'But I'm the best one I know and my mum is backup if I need it. Right now I'm going into my room to take a shower. It might not be a bad idea if you did the same—you look pretty awful,' she lied.

Dragging a hand across his stubble-roughened jaw, he regarded her with an expression of stark incredulity. 'You can't close the door on this or me.'

'I know that, I just... Why *did* you come here like this—for me to apologise for having Emmy?' She lifted her chin and shook her head. 'It's *never* going to happen, and even if I had told you I'd have never let you convince me to have a termination.'

'Is that what you think I'd have done?' A look of stark incredulity spread across his lean face as her comment sank in. 'Is that why you didn't tell me?'

'I had enough to contend with without having to fight with you too.' She closed her eyes, a brief respite from the intensity of his cobalt stare. She tightened the hold on her towel before continuing in a slow, carefully controlled voice. 'I know you don't want children. It's not like it's a secret. That's your choice. Mine was to have Emmy.' There had been enough voices that suggested she shouldn't, without adding another.

'You think I would have coerced you?' He struggled to hide how much the idea shocked him.

'It was not your choice to make,' she said evenly. 'But don't try and tell me you'd have been happy if you'd known about Emmy. We had casual sex and I got pregnant. Everything that happened after that was my choice, my responsibility.'

'What world do you live in that you think *my* child is not my responsibility? I could have walked past my own daughter on the street and not known who she was...' He closed his eyes and let the pent-up breath in his chest escape before fixing her with a steady look of intent and warning. 'If you think I'm going to walk away now, forget it. It's not going to happen and all the talk and protests and blame-laying is not going to change that.'

Lily's chin lifted. 'I might have been wrong not to tell you about Emmy—'

'Might?'

'You're looking for a reason to be mad with me!' she charged.

His pressed the heels of his hands to his brow and shook his head slowly.

'It's true! But you have no right to—'

His hands fell away and landed on her shoulders. Enough was enough. 'Look at me...'

She struggled with all her might to resist his demand, but the compulsion was too strong. 'I have rights. You may wish it otherwise, but I am the child's father and I intend to play a part in her life.'

His hands fell away and Lily's slender shoulders sagged in defeat. 'So what happens now?'

Good question. 'We talk. I'll pick you up at...' he

glanced at his watch and thought a moment before adding
'...seven. In the hotel foyer?'

Too drained to argue, she watched him go before
turning and entering her bungalow.

She flung herself face down on the sofa and, feeling
emotionally battered, cried herself to sleep.

CHAPTER THREE

SHE WAS STILL lying there several hours later when the maid brought her some afternoon tea.

'Are you all right, miss?'

Lily pulled herself upright and pressed a hand to her head. 'I had a headache, Mathilde.' It was no lie; her head was pounding.

The maid made sympathetic noises and carried on chatting as Lily went off in search of an aspirin for her pounding head. Finding some in her flight bag, she swallowed them down. The scene from earlier replayed in her head as she washed her face and smoothed down her hair with a hand before returning.

The maid was still there emanating an air of barely suppressed excitement, which was explained when she tipped her glossy head towards the tray. 'You have an important message, miss, right there.'

Lily opened the blank envelope that lay on the plate beside the basket of bite-sized savoury scones and sandwiches. Aware of the curious eyes trained on her face, she slid out the single sheet of hotel headed notepaper inside and unfolded it, and read it.

Six-thirty.

A man of few words and none of them *please*, she thought, experiencing a stab of rebellion, before reality kicked in and she thought, *What's the point? Save your energy for the battles that matter.* A change of schedule was not one of them.

'The man who left it at Reception is the rich Englishman,' the maid explained, her eyes alive with curiosity.

'Not all Englishmen are rich, Mathilde.'

'*He* is,' the girl insisted. 'He arrived on a private plane this morning and it's still sitting on the runway. The flight crew are staying on the other side of the island. I know because my cousin works at the hotel. The Englishman pays their wages while they sunbathe and eat their heads off. *That*,' she said firmly, 'is rich.'

Lily could not argue. And being *that* rich was usually equated with power, she reminded herself. A fact she had been in danger of forgetting, not that it was exactly news. The family at the big house were not exactly poor, but since he had first appeared in the Top 100 Rich List five years ago Benedict Warrender's name had been climbing, while his number of visits to the estate had fallen.

'So is he your boyfriend?'

It wasn't hard to laugh at the description or ignore the dish-the-dirt invitation.

'No, he isn't.' She felt almost guilty when the other girl's face fell. 'We really don't live in the same world. My mother works for his family, my father used to as well.' Lily felt a wistful stab of nostalgia for the time when their connection had been that simple and straightforward. But at least, fingers crossed, she had killed off any rumours that might be circulating on the island.

She kept the maid talking, delaying the moment when she would be alone with her own thoughts and fears. But inevitably it came.

Lily spent the rest of the day in a state of nervous anticipation. She would obviously have to compromise, but how much…?

She was ready early, too early. Luckily her holiday wardrobe was limited so by the time she took a last look in the mirror she had only changed outfit three times. Then she was almost late when, halfway to the main hotel building, she realised she'd forgotten her shoes. By the time she finally entered the main hotel build-ing carrying a pair of pretty sparkly sandals, she felt hot and breathless.

Her eyes went to the clock on the wall: still early. *Why does it matter if you're late?* she asked herself as she dusted the sand off her feet and slipped on the san-dals. What she would have given to have had a pair of confidence-boosting killer heels with her. Chasing round after a two-year-old meant that heels were things of the past for Lily and, as she'd been coming on this holiday alone, it hadn't occurred to her to pack anything other than beach footwear.

'Miss Gray.'

Lily straightened up to face the girl who had emerged from behind Reception.

'Mr Warrender said to tell you he will be outside at six-thirty.'

In case I couldn't read. 'Thank you.'

'Can I get you a cocktail?'

'Yes,' Lily said, feeling in desperate need of some Dutch courage for the unknown road that lay ahead.

* * *

She was outside waiting when he drew up in an open-topped, luxury four-wheel drive. Sitting in the driver's seat, his short hair ruffled by the wind, he looked casual and elegant in an open-necked white shirt and pale biscuit linen trousers; a matching jacket lay folded on the back seat.

A hotel doorman hurried over to open the door for her. The high step into the vehicle meant she was glad of his helping hand.

As she got in beside him the nervous tension he had picked up on from a distance was more pronounced. Not the first thing he noticed about her, of course. He felt heat slither through his body leaving a molten trail that pooled hotly in his groin before he looked away.

'Sorry if you were expecting a limo—'

'I wasn't,' she said in a voice that lacked all intonation. 'Where are we going?'

'Someone recommended a place close by, but apparently the roads this side of the island require a four-wheel drive so—' He left the sentence incomplete and looked at her hard for longer than was polite. She didn't turn her head but she could feel his stare.

She was taken aback when he said, almost accusingly, 'You smell of something…flowers…?'

She raised her arm to her face and held the inner aspect of her wrist to her nose, only getting the faintest suggestion of rose. He must have an ultra-sensitive nose or maybe he just hated the light citrusy perfume. Her slender shoulders lifted. 'My soap.' It was one she had used since she was a little girl.

She had used it that night and left the scent on the pillow, Ben thought.

As she struggled with her seat belt he turned his head, his hungry glance taking in the tumble of her glorious burnished loose hair swept over one shoulder. She was wearing a green dress that exposed her beautiful collarbones, shoulders and the delicate curve of her upper spine. As she leaned a little more forward adjusting her seat belt, her silky hair slithered around her face, revealing her neck. He turned his head sharply. When he began to fantasise about the back of a woman's neck it was time to—to what exactly? He shook himself. He was here to negotiate custody terms, not sex.

It was not going to be easy and Ben knew he could not afford to blur the lines or allow himself to be distracted. It was basic logic in the art of negotiation.

'Sorry I'm early.' He glanced in the rear-view mirror and pulled out between the palms.

'You weren't. I got the note *and* the message.'

The tetchy note raised a lopsided grin. 'I don't like to be kept waiting.'

'Now there's a surprise.'

'I suggest you hang on.'

She ignored the comment but a couple of minutes later decided to put safety above pride and grabbed hold of the handrail.

'I'm told there won't be enough room outside the place to park,' Ben explained as he pulled the car up a short while later within sight of a magically pretty harbour. 'Can your heels cope with the cobbles?'

Struggling not to react as she felt his eyes on her legs, Lily brushed her hand up and down the skirt of

the green halter-necked dress she wore before she un-
crossed her ankles.

'I'm not wearing heels. I'll be fine,' she said, thinking, *This was such a bad idea.* 'I wasn't expecting dinner or—'

'Neutral territory seemed like a good idea,' he returned smoothly. 'And we have to eat. Relax, it's not
a date.'

'I never thought it was.' She jumped down unaided
before he made it around to her side. He held out a hand
to help her regain her balance after her foot caught in
a pothole. The road was littered with them. That was
what had made the journey so bumpy—the last half-
mile had been on a dirt track.

Lily conspicuously avoided his hand and eased her
spine straight. She felt as though she had been riding
a bucking bronco, but on the plus side negotiating the
road with its hair-pin bends and the occasional oncom-
ing vehicle on the wrong side of the road had meant
he wasn't inclined to make conversation. All that had
changed: now she faced an evening of careful negotiation, of compromise.

She couldn't afford to relax her guard for an instant,
Lily reminded herself as she lifted her chin. She would
not be bullied; this was going to be on her terms.

As they began to walk down the hill there was a loud
blast of laughter from the harbour area. Lily turned her
head in response to the sound. In the moonlight her
delicate cut-glass profile made Ben catch his breath as,
slim and graceful, she stepped ahead.

He lengthened his stride and, conscious of his presence beside her, Lily lost the fight against the compulsion to look up at him. In the darkness his face was all

angles and planes. She looked away quickly, afraid that he'd see the shameful ache of hunger she felt when she looked at him.

'Careful, this bit is steep.' He caught her elbow, seeing her eyes widen revealingly at the contact that sent an electric thrill through his body too. 'So how was it?'

'What?'

'Your massage.'

With no warning an image scrolled through her head, hands strong and brown, clever long fingers kneading her flesh, and she almost stumbled. It would have taken more than a massage to iron out the knots in her neck and shoulders.

'Very relaxing,' she lied.

The cobbled surface became more even as they entered the harbour. The transition from the empty road, fringed by rain forest, to the lively little harbour, strung with coloured lanterns and lined with cafés and bars, was abrupt. The laid-back café atmosphere was a world away from the luxurious but carefully manicured world of the hotel. Lily preferred it—or she would have, had the circumstances that brought her here been less fraught.

Ben led her directly to a restaurant that had tables set out on a platform over the water.

'I thought you'd like to sit outside?' he said as they were led by a smiling waiter to a relatively private table at the water's edge. Muted sounds of jazz playing from inside mingled with the sound of the water lapping against the harbour wall. It was relaxing. 'Apparently the food is good.'

She huffed an impatient sigh. Why was he pretending this was civilised? 'I'm not hungry.'

Elbows resting on the table, he leaned forward. It was a small table and their knees almost touched under it. Lily fought the urge to lean back; instead she sat bolt upright in her chair.

'This doesn't have to be so hard.'

Without warning, a fly-on-the-wall image of herself sitting astride Ben, her hands on his hot, damp skin, drawing hoarse cries from his parted lips, flashed into her head. She pressed a hand to her throat, felt the sweat pool in the hollow between her breasts and picked up the menu, wishing it were big enough to hide behind.

'I'm not hungry,' she repeated flatly.

He shrugged and sat back. 'Suit yourself.'

She watched, indignant that he seemed so relaxed, as he calmly scanned the menu. It appeared to be written entirely in French, and he ordered in the same language.

Connecting with the smoky green eyes regarding him with hostile suspicion above the menu, Ben arched a brow.

'I'll just have a salad,' she said to the waiter.

Ben waited until the young man had left before saying, 'I've spoken to my lawyer.'

The word sent alarm bells off. Thoughts of custody battles spinning through her head, she pulled herself back from the brink of panic.

'Water?'

She nodded and ran her tongue across her dry lips. 'Please,' and added, *'Lawyer?'*

'He's making the necessary changes to my will.'

She looked at him blankly as he began to fill his own glass from the iced bottle on the table. 'I don't understand.'

'I'm not planning on dying tomorrow or any time soon, but should something happen...'

He sat there looking more vital and alive than any person on the planet. She nipped in a quick breath but it didn't lessen the compressing band around her chest. She couldn't think anything at all beyond a total rejection of a world that didn't have this man in it.

'I'm being practical.'

I hate practical, she thought.

'I need to make provisions,' he said, perfectly aware that he had flung himself headlong into the practicalities of his new role because it delayed the moment when he'd have to face up to the other aspects—aspects he felt unqualified to tackle.

Could love be learnt? Or were the experts who claimed that a person who'd not been loved as a child could never feel that emotion in their own life right?

He pushed aside the questions in his head and continued. 'Oh, and the trust fund, they can run the details past you next. I'm assuming that you would like to be one of the trustees?'

With all the talk of trust funds and wills, Lily's head had started to spin. 'This is all very—' She looked at him with a frown and shook her head. 'I thought you'd want to ask me questions...'

'About what?' He pretended not to understand the *you've got to be joking* look she slung him.

'Emmy.' Her frown deepened as she struggled to name the emotion she had seen flicker in his eyes before they shuttered and the blue surface showed nothing but her own reflection. 'Don't you want to know about her?'

'I don't know much about babies...she seemed to

have all the right bits in the right places...' he said, feeling as lame as he knew he sounded. 'I know she has a good set of lungs.'

The inspired observation made her smile, then a moment later she stiffened. 'How? How do you know?'

It was not difficult to see that her imagination was running riot. 'I saw her, remember.'

'And she was crying? Why...what?'

'Don't panic!' He put his hands up in a calming gesture. She had leaned forward in her seat and looked ready to throttle the information out of him if he didn't cough it up. 'She'd fallen and bumped her head, chasing a cat, I think.' His hand went to his throat. 'She ate my tie.' His blue eyes softened at the memory.

Lily leaned back in her seat. 'Everything goes in her mouth.' She caught herself smiling and stopped. 'So what's the deal here, then? Do you want to spend time with her?'

'Of course I do. She's mine, I'd like to get to know her.'

'A child takes up a lot of time, and you have a very busy schedule.' It didn't seem like a massive leap to make; a man didn't reach his position unless he was a bit of a workaholic.

Ice formed in his expression as he listened to her. 'Are you trying to suggest that I'd put my work ahead of my child?'

She looked surprised by the question. 'It wouldn't make you unique, but what I'm actually trying to say is that people don't realise how much hard work a small child can be...even if it is just for the odd weekend.' She dropped the napkin she had been twisting between her fingers, as the mental door she had closed against speculation opened another inch. 'When you look after her, will you have a nanny?' It seemed a massive extravagance to Lily for the handful of hours involved, but then he could afford it. 'If you do, I'd like to be part of that choice.'

'So you've no objection to nannies?'

'Better a nanny than your latest girlfriend.'

'So you want to be part of that choice too? Or am I to be celibate?'

'Laugh if you want but—'

'Relax. I want to get to know my daughter without third parties.'

Would there come a time when he would consider *her* an intrusive third party? The panic inside her grew until she was within a second of telling him she'd changed her mind, that she wasn't agreeing to anything at all. But then his calm voice cut through her inner turmoil.

'I'm not trying to kidnap her, you know. I just want to be part of her life. I want—' He paused and thought, *What? What do you want, Ben?* The answer, when it came to him, made him relax back in his seat. 'I want her to know that if she ever needs me I'll be there.'

There was no question that he was genuine. He would be there for Emmy. *And that was something I was going to deny her?* Suddenly overwhelmed by a tide of guilt, Lily looked away.

'You sure about the salad?'

Lily looked up. 'What?'

Ben was watching a platter of seafood being whisked past the table. 'That looks really good.'

'I'm really not hungry.'

'Do you want me to be there when you tell your mother?'

The suggestion made her eyes fly wide. 'No, I don't! I hadn't even thought about telling her.'

He laid down his glass. 'I really don't think that's an option, do you?'

'No...yes...there's no need to go public with this, is there? It's private.'

Ben's jaw clenched as he guessed that by private she actually meant secret. 'Oh, no, I want you to send me report cards and...' He gave a contemptuous grimace. 'Of course I want to "go public", as you put it. After I've broken the news to my grandfather, that is.'

Lily leaned back in her chair. 'Oh, God!'

'Oh, he'll be delighted. Once he gets over the fact he's been living half a mile from his granddaughter for two years. Two years he's missed out on.'

Lily lowered her gaze from his expression. It was obvious that Ben was no longer talking about his grandfather.

'Everything is going to change,' she realised.

He was never going to forgive her. With a sinking heart she recognised the fact that this much, at least, would never change.

She looked up and saw the mockery in his blue eyes. 'You catch on quick. Tell me, what did you *think* was going to happen?'

'I suppose...' She swallowed and gave an unhappy little shrug. 'I thought we could go slowly...you could see Emmy with me there at first for an hour or so. Later maybe, when she got to know you, take her to the park or something. I thought we were going to talk some more and discuss things...'

'We are—we have been.'

She shook her head. 'No,' she denied. 'We are not

talking. You are *telling* me, not asking.' The waiter appeared and she waited while the food was set down before adding, 'There's been no discussion.'

'So what do you want to discuss?'

Lily looked at him in seething frustration as she tried to organise her thoughts. 'This is too much too fast. You might change your mind. I don't want Emmy to get to know you, only to have you disappear from her life. She needs stability, continuity...not—'

'She needs a father. I get it that you think I'm some sort of low life...'

'I didn't say that!' she protested, watching him dissect the steak on his plate.

He laid down his knife and looked up at her, his steely gaze as unrelenting as a surgical scalpel.

'It isn't going to happen.' His jaw line tightened as he spelt out his intention. 'Lily, I'm going to be part of my daughter's life so get used to it. I'm in this for the long haul.'

His take-it-or-leave-it stance made her feel angry and helpless.

'You say that now,' she countered, dropping the fork she was stirring her salad with and glaring at him. 'But your track record doesn't inspire confidence. And I have to protect my daughter.'

His dark brows lifted. 'Care to elaborate?' he drawled.

'Well, I expect you told the woman—the one you were engaged to when you slept with me—that you were in it for the long haul...?'

To her amazement some of the tension left his jaw; he actually laughed. 'Caro...?'

'Was there more than one?' she asked sourly.

'We were never actually engaged.'

This display of deceit sparked her anger into life. 'I saw the ring!' she exclaimed contemptuously.

His ex had been wearing the ring in several of the photos accompanying the article.

'There was a ring, granted. But it was a gift.'

Anger boomed in her head like a pulse. She pressed her fingers to her temple and realised it actually was her pulse. 'So she imagined the engagement, then?'

Her thinly veiled sarcasm drew a calm response. 'No, she invented it.'

'As you do.'

'You had to be there,' he drawled, thinking of the nightclub Caro had dragged him to. With the music booming, it was usually the sort of place that he avoided.

He'd even been amused when she'd transferred the ring he'd bought her to her left hand. Then he'd seen the paparazzi and realised it was a set-up—*he'd* been set up. You had to admire her ingenuity and she hadn't even tried to deny it.

'Do you know how many cookbooks get published in a year? Even the novelty value of me being an ex-model will only get me so far... Being dumped by a heartless billionaire?' She had produced a mock sad face before delivering an equally brilliant smile and adding, 'It will raise my profile.'

'And sell books.'

'Obviously. But I was thinking more of a TV show. That's where the real money is.'

That was what he'd liked about Caro: she'd never pretended. That and her appetite for sex.

'So we're splitting up?'

'You're heartbroken. I can tell. Honestly, I don't want to, but a girl has to make a living.'

He shook his head as the formerly meaningless memories faded. Now he realised that the implication that he'd been engaged had stopped Lily from telling him she was pregnant.

'I was there, remember?' Lily bit back. 'I was the other woman.'

He stared at her and looked thoughtful. 'And that bothers you?'

Her cheeks grew pink. 'As a matter of fact, yes, it does.'

'If you mind so much, it might be a good idea in future to ask a few questions before you jump into bed with someone.'

Indignant, she sat bolt upright in her chair. 'Talk about double standards. I don't recall you asking me many questions. For all you knew I might have had a boyfriend.'

'Oh, I'm not trying to occupy the moral high ground,' he retorted. 'Though I have to admit, skipping out while my partner is asleep has never been my style.'

Feeling the flush mounting in her cheeks, she lowered her gaze and grabbed her glass.

'It wouldn't have mattered anyway. *I had to have you.*'

The sudden raw, throaty admission brought her eyes up. She had barely registered the dark feral gleam in his eyes before it was gone. Then he picked up the threads of their previous conversation as though nothing had happened.

'So do you want me to be with you when you tell your mother or not?'

'Tell my mother?' Had she imagined it? The heat between her thighs was not imaginary.

'Well, we're not telling mine.'

'Why not?'

'Signe has been known to forget she has a son. I seriously doubt she'll be interested in a grandchild.'

It took her a moment to place the name. He called his mother by her Christian name. 'No, seriously—'

'Yes, seriously. She is not the most family-orientated woman in the world. Sadly I inherited that much from her, so this is going to be a learning curve for me.'

The admission surprised her.

'You sound like… Do you *dislike* her, your mother?' He did not seem offended by the question. It seemed to her he was actually thinking about it.

'Not dislike, no. We are not close and I actually admire her achievements. She has carved out a niche in the world of international law—small world, smaller niche, but she is the undisputed authority.'

'She's your mother.' Lily was shocked by the objective analysis. 'You sound as though you're talking about a stranger.'

'We don't all get given the perfect family, like you had.'

'My family wasn't perfect. My dad…' She stopped, mortified to feel her eyes fill with tears.

'Sorry. I remember your father.' From somewhere he retrieved a memory; it was pleasant. 'One Christmas when we were staying at Warren Court, before I moved in, he taught me to fish.'

'Did he? I didn't know that.'

'He was really one of the good guys.'

'You sound like my mum. She always talks about the past as though it was perfect, glowing and golden, never a cross word. Truth is they used to fight all the time. I hated it—it made me feel…not safe.'

She stopped before she poured out anything further. *Why on earth had she said those things to him of all people?* It was not even something she had discussed with her twin.

'I suppose it is a matter of interpretation. For me it was the silences, the apathy when people can't be bothered to fight. That's when a relationship is dead. Conflict can be healthy.'

She gave a snort of disbelief.

'For what it's worth your parents always seemed passionately in love to me. They sparked off one another.' Before she could respond, he reached across and speared a slice of avocado from her plate with his fork, studying her face. 'But then it's not a subject I'm an expert on.'

'Have it if you want,' she said, pushing her plate towards him when he appropriated some more.

'I will. I've not had time to eat and the only food in the house was a cupboard of tinned peaches.'

'House?'

'It turns out I have one here.'

'Turns out?'

'I had an uncle who lived here—you know about the Danish connection?'

She nodded. 'Someone mentioned it.'

'He died last year.'

'Sorry.'

'I never met him. Signe is not big into keeping family connections. Well, I inherited the place and I never got around to putting it on the market. It's in the old part of town.'

'The conservation area?' She had walked past the big old houses and been charmed.

He nodded. 'I'd invite you over but the dust is inches thick.'

'So he was all alone?'

'With a house full of memories.'

'That's so sad.'

He was twisting the lid off a bottle of iced water. He had long, elegant fingers, deft and strong. She could remember how strong and how sensitive. Tactile images rushed in, threatening to drag her back. She struggled to banish them, but not before she had relived the moment his hand had closed around one breast, cupping it in his palm.

'I should have asked if you wanted wine. I'm the designated driver.' He held her eyes as he poured the water over the chinking ice in his frosted glass, then, lifting it in a silent toast, he looked at her through the glass.

'I don't.' The last thing she needed was her inhibitions loosening.

'Well, cheers to me.'

She looked at him, her brow furrowed.

'It's my birthday.'

'Seriously?'

He arched a satirical brow. The emotions that lay just below the smile in his eyes sent a deep shiver rippling through her body, like the silver light on the moonlit sea.

'I'd forgotten.'

'How can you forget your birthday?' In her family birthdays were a big deal. Last year was the first one that she and Lara had not celebrated together.

'A lot of things have been happening.'

'Well, happy birthday.' It sounded inane.

He responded with a tilt of his head. 'It is certainly one I won't forget.'

'What did you do on your last birthday?'

'Actually I do remember that one. I spent it in bed.'

CHAPTER FOUR

'You were ill?'

There was a moment's startled silence that was broken by his laughter. It was pitched low but an unexpected lull in the conversation on the tables around them had made the sound travel.

'Then why were you—?' she began, then stopped, her eyes flying wide as understanding dawned. The hot mortified colour flew to her cheeks and with it came a breath-catching knife thrust of concentrated corrosive jealousy.

The blush fascinated him... Did it go all over? His eyes dropped, the laughter fading from his face replaced by something much harder as his glance fell and lingered on the upper slopes of her breasts, where they strained against the silky green fabric.

Lily reacted to his glance as if it were a caress. She had zero control over the reaction of her disastrously receptive body to the brush of his eyes and she lifted her hand far too late to hide it from him.

'Oh.'

The sound that left his throat this time was more growl than laugh. It made the fine downy hairs on her body lift from her sensitised skin. When his eyes lifted and levelled on hers, they were several shades darker.

'Relax. I've never expected a woman to sleep with me for the price of a dinner.' He lifted his glass with a clink of ice. 'That's not to say an evening hasn't occasionally concluded that way,' he drawled provocatively.

'I can imagine,' she snapped back and lifted her chin, unwittingly drawing his attention to the long, lovely line of her graceful neck. 'So long as you know that this one isn't.' In her head the delivery had been amused but to her frustration when it actually left her lips the comment was throaty...a little breathless.

His thoughts swung back to earlier when he had arrived at the hotel just as she'd emerged. That traffic-stopping dress that hugged the curves of her body and the long, sinuous line of her endless legs.

Unable to control the consequences of the testosterone rush her emergence had produced, he had been forced to remain in his seat and let her climb in with the help of the porter.

For a man who prided himself on his self-control the drive to the harbour restaurant had been new territory. Rather than subside, his painful arousal had become excruciating when she'd slid in beside him. She'd smelled delicious. And he'd itched to touch the silk of her dress and everything beneath...

It had taken the rest of the journey to get his libido in check—not that the hunger had gone away. His lowered heavy lids did not completely hide the gleam in his eyes as he studied her, trying to work out what it was about her. Beyond the blindingly obvious—this was way more than her looking like an advert for sin—what was it that made him feel so out of control?

Just when he needed it, his ability to see beyond his own emotional reaction to a situation and apply clear-headed logic deserted him. He inhaled and dragged his eyes clear of the sensuous soft trembling outline of her lips and growled a soft warning.

'Be careful, Lily, some men might take that as a challenge.'

Lily, who was already regretting the comment that had invited his response, shook her head and kept her voice carefully flat as she responded, 'It wasn't.'

Hands clenched, she dabbed her tongue to the beads of sweat along her upper lip. She could control her voice, but her traitorous thoughts were another matter entirely.

And *this* definitely wasn't what she wanted, she reminded herself as she studied the tablecloth. Some complications she had no control over; this was one she did. All it required was a little willpower, a little self-control.

Emmy was their link; their roles as her parents needed to be strictly defined.

The only problem was that when he looked at her *that* way her self-control went on holiday.

The first challenge was to hide the chain reaction that had begun as a tremor in the pit of her belly. It was now spreading until her skin was prickling with sensation and she was shaking inside and out. It was terrifying to feel this much and he wasn't even touching her.

'I thought it might be my birthday present.' His voice was light, but the accompanying gleam in his eyes was anything but.

She shook out her napkin and dabbed her lips. 'I wonder where the ladies' room is?' she said, following up her comment with an ostentatious glance over each shoulder.

She had half risen to her feet when her glance connected with his. Without warning her knees folded and she sat down with a gentle thud. The explicit gleam of hunger in his eyes had a paralysing effect.

Without breaking eye contact he clicked his long fingers.

'Bill, please.'

Lily watched through her lashes as he placed a wad of notes on the plate, not even looking at the denominations, though from the waiter's expression there were way too many.

'We're going?'

He arched a dark brow. 'You want to stay?'

Lily looked at him and wished she didn't know what she wanted. 'I thought you were hungry.'

'I am.'

Their glances connected, startled green on smouldering blue, and though her insides dissolved she ignored the sensation and didn't ask him to explain the comment. She already knew and to admit it would have made the return journey more awkward. It was easier to ignore the elephant in the room.

As it was they completed the trip in total silence and to hear him finally break it made her start violently.

'We're here.'

Ben pulled the car to a halt; without the engine noise everything seemed very quiet. She could hear her own heartbeat and the distant sound of the ocean.

Disorientated, she looked around. 'But—' She stopped, realising that he hadn't driven through the main gates. He'd turned the vehicle down a dirt track that came to a dead end in the trees. Through the leafy canopy she could make out the outline of her bungalow.

'Right, thanks.'

'I wanted to ask something…'

Her heart started to thud; in the darkness his blue eyes were hypnotically dark. A wave of longing rolled over her, blanking all logical thought. 'What?'

'I wondered if you had a photo of Emily Rose that I could have?'

And straight away she was back to reality. He was thinking about Emmy and she… Lily's skin burned with mortified heat as she tipped her head. She was just relieved that she hadn't lunged at him like some sex-starved teenager. 'Of course, I brought some with me.'

'I'll stop by tomorrow to pick it up. Have a think about what we've discussed. You can tell me how you feel about what I've said tonight… I don't want you to feel that I'm pushing you.'

'Yes, that would be…' she took a deep breath '…fine.'

She closed her eyes and stayed where she was, calling herself all kinds of fool, while he walked around to her side of the car.

Without the headlights it was dark, but as he reached the passenger side a shaft of moonlight pierced the leafy canopy, picking out the slim figure poised to jump down.

A deep breath rattled deep in his chest. The light shone straight through the green fluttering dress, outlining the sinuous softness of her slim body, and simultaneously lust slammed through him.

It was a bad idea on more levels than he could count. But this was not about right or wrong, it was about the hunger seeping into every cell of his body—some more than others!

He knew the sex would be great—more than great—but then what…?

How many excellent working relationships had he seen go bad because the people involved fell into bed? When things went wrong, as they inevitably did, the recriminations and the name-calling started… Hell, no, nightmare! He had to think long term. It was going to be hard enough to establish a relationship with his daughter without adding any more obstacles.

'Careful, there's a bit of a hole here.' He held out his arms and she automatically stepped into them.

Her timing was slightly off and the collision that made him take a step back caused the breath to exit her lungs in a soft whoosh as their bodies connected. 'Sorry,' she mumbled.

His response was to draw her closer to his body until she was plastered up against him like a second skin. She was painfully aware of the rock-hard imprint of his erection in her belly. A small whimper left her lips as she pressed her face for a moment into his shoulder and, squeezing her eyes closed, stayed there.

'You all right?' He curved a big hand around her face, drawing it up to him.

The *almost* tenderness in his voice filled her throat with emotion. Combined with the hot lust pumping through her veins, it rendered her dumb and pliable as a marionette.

His breathing got louder and faster as she tapped into hidden reserves and drew back a little.

'This is a bad idea, Ben,' she whispered, thinking it was more than bad—insane really.

As if things weren't complicated enough.

'Agreed.' He nodded, tightening his arm around her ribcage. 'Bad idea…'

Lily didn't fight the constraint. Instead she lifted the hand that was not trapped between her body and him and touched the hard, abrasive angle of his jaw. 'Really bad.' Stretching her body up in an arc, she pressed a hard kiss on his mouth.

He let out a low half-growl, half-moan and then released her. He grabbed her hand and headed to the bungalow. Unable to keep up with his long-legged pace, Lily had to trot alongside panting.

They arrived at the bungalow hand in hand and breathless. He turned and looked at her, the raw desire written into the hard lines of his face, and the hungry glow in his eyes made her insides dissolve. Lily closed her eyes and whimpered, feeling the brush of his lips on her eyelids before he scooped her up and carried her inside.

Kicking the door closed behind them, Ben looked around. 'Where's the bed?'

'It doesn't matter,' she murmured indistinctly.

Ben nodded and sank down to the floor with her in his arms; kneeling, he laid her down. Lily lay there on the polished boards, her breasts lifting in time to her uneven, laboured breathing. A strange enervating weakness seemed to have invaded her limbs. The entire surface of her body prickled with a sensual awareness. One arm flung above her head, the other held in a tight clenched fist on her chest, she watched through half-closed eyes as he knelt over her and fought his way out of his shirt.

The rippling perfection of his taut, lean body took

her breath away and pushed her deeper into the sensual vortex of her own desire. He looked like some pagan god.

'You're so beautiful!' She struggled to force the words past the aching occlusion in her throat. She reached up and ran her fingers down the hair-roughened ridge of his ribbed belly, then, hooking her fingers into the waistband of his linen trousers, she pulled him down.

Ben, a dark slash of colour crossing the contours of his cheekbones, slid one hand under her lower back to cushion the impact as his body pushed her into the ground. With a grunt he rolled her onto her side so that they were facing each other.

She could feel his hands shaking as he reached for the tie on her halter dress. She was shaking all over too. She lay there weak with wanting as he kissed his way down the curve of her neck. When he reached the pulsing hollow at the base of her throat, he peeled down the top to her waist, exposing her breasts.

He gave a long shuddering sigh that seemed to be wrenched from deep inside him. 'So beautiful, Lily.' Her femininity touched him in a deep place. He didn't think of it as his soul; it would make this something it wasn't… Sex, this was just sex—great sex, granted. 'You're so totally…' Lost for words, he made his kisses speak for him.

The wild onslaught took her breath away. Limbs locked, mouths sealed, they kissed with a frantic, wild abandon until Ben levered himself off her and reached for the button on his trousers.

Anxious to be rid of the barrier between them, she lifted her hips to slide the dress down over them. Before she had managed to wriggle free there was a sound. She didn't register it at first…and then as the noise penetrated the layers of sexual thrall that gripped her, she stopped and looked around.

What was she doing?

The journey from hot, passionate arousal to cold, horrified self-disgust took a single heartbeat. She pulled herself onto her knees and sat there, her arms crossed over her bare breasts.

'What the hell…?' Breathing hard, the testosterone in his blood still surging painfully through his body, he struggled to make sense of what was happening. She'd been with him every step of the way; he knew she had. So what had changed?

There was another knock on the door. This time he heard it too.

Without looking at him, Lily pulled the bodice of her dress up and tied it. She walked across the room and paused at the door, smoothing her hair before taking a deep breath. She opened it and immediately stepped outside, quickly closing it behind her to hide Ben from the person standing there.

It was the hotel manager. Her smile faded the moment she saw his face illuminated by the overhead light. At her sides her hands clenched.

'What's wrong?'

'Nothing to worry about.'

The jovial assurance filled her with instant trepidation.

'Your mother has been trying to contact you. As you probably know we have had a problem with the

Internet connection, so she left a message for you to contact her.'

Alarm bells ringing a deafening peal in her head, Lily resisted the tug of total panic, though her voice sounded unnaturally shrill to her ears as she asked, 'Now?'

The man looked relieved that she wasn't panicking. If only he knew!

'If you'd like to use the landline? My office is at your disposal.'

Lily, her heart thudding sickly, nodded. 'I'll just get my jacket.'

The man walked down the steps as she nipped back inside. She closed the door and leaned against it, eyes shut.

'What's wrong?' Bare-chested, Ben walked across the room; the frustration that had gripped him had vanished the moment he saw her.

Lily opened her eyes and looked at him blankly. It seemed to him almost as though she had forgotten he was there.

'I don't know,' she said, peeling her back from the door. 'But apparently my mother has been trying to contact me. There's no mobile signal and the Internet has been playing up so I'm going to the hotel to call her back.'

'Don't overreact,' he advised. 'It might be nothing.'

She rounded on him, eyes blazing. 'Of course it's something. Don't patronise me.'

'Emily Rose?'

Icily composed now, she nodded. 'Probably.' Her daughter needed her, and she'd been... She pressed a hand to her stomach as self-loathing made the muscles tighten and she pushed through a wave of nausea.

Ben reached for his shirt, his eyes on her paper-pale face as he dressed. 'I'll come with you.'

Lily's chin had dropped on her chest but came up sharply now as she blurted forcefully, 'No!'

The rejection hit him at a level he didn't analyse, but there was pain involved. 'You can't be alone—'

'I've been alone for three years.'

Ben flinched.

'I need to do this alone.'

There was a pause before he tilted his head in acknowledgement. 'I'll be here if you need me.'

'Thanks, but it's probably nothing,' she said, her laugh brittle. 'Mum's probably lost her favourite toy and she won't go to sleep without it.'

'You're probably right, but I'll hang around until you get back, if that's all right?'

'There's really no need.'

'There's really no need for you to do this alone,' he countered.

She lifted her chin. 'It's what I do.'

Ben watched as she joined the suited figure waiting on the path. He stayed there until they were swallowed up by shadows.

Frustration gnawed at him as he began to pace the room. The calm detachment with which he tackled difficult moments eluded him. Her rejection of his assistance had got to him more than he was prepared to admit. Was she trying to prove a point...to herself...to him? He had no idea; he just wished she'd not chosen this moment to do it.

As the minutes ticked by he kept seeing her scared face, feeling the same rush of unaccustomed protectiveness that had taken him totally unawares...and her efforts to put a brave face on it when she was clearly terrified... What if it turned out she had reason to be?

Ben managed to contain his frustration for five minutes before he followed her. She didn't want his help? Too bad, she had it.

He stopped short of actually entering the building, contenting himself with waiting outside. He had worn a path in the greenery by the time she appeared.

He raised a hand and after a short pause Lily walked across to him.

Her face, pale and strained, said it all.

'I need to get back to England.'

'Is it...?'

'Emmy has been admitted to hospital.'

'What happened? Did she fall? Is there anything broken?'

'No. She's ill. I don't know what with. She's ill and I need to get home, that's all I know. But it's a bank holiday or something and there isn't a spare seat on any flight until Monday.' Hearing the husky tremor in her voice, she swallowed and lifted her chin. 'You came in a private plane?'

She saw the anger flare in his eyes and misinterpreted it.

'I wouldn't ask but...'

She was asking, *that* was the point. She was acting as though he needed to be asked. As though he needed to be persuaded to help when his daughter was ill.

He reached into his trouser pocket, pulled out his phone and began to punch in numbers. He lifted a finger, said, 'Give me a minute,' and turned away.

Lily watched as he walked a few yards away and then began to pace back and forth as he spoke into his phone. The conversation did not last long before he slid it back into his pocket and joined her.

'I'll pick you up in an hour. Tell your mother we should be there by breakfast.'

She expelled a deep sigh of relief. 'That's…' She moved forward to embrace him, but something in his expression stopped her.

'You don't need to thank me or be grateful, Lily. She's my daughter too.'

Aware she had offended him but too preoccupied to figure out how or why, she nodded and said, 'An hour?'

The vagueness in her voice brought his searching scrutiny to her face. What he saw there made him catch hold of her hands and pull her around to face him. He didn't have to be an expert to recognise shock when he saw it.

'You need to… *Lily*…!' The sound of her name drew Lily's green, oddly flat stare up to his. Through his hold on her narrow, delicate wrists, he could feel the tremors that were striking intermittently through her body. Ben took a deep breath and spoke slowly. 'You need to pack and…' He stopped. Two things were obvious: she was not listening, or at least not *hearing* him, and he was way out of his depth. Being excluded was bad but this… This, he decided, was way worse.

Lily looked at him and thought, *Why is he telling me this? Does he think I'm stupid or something?*

'It's fine. I'll sort it.'

He led her back to the bungalow, emptied a miniature of brandy from the bar into a glass, stood over her while she swallowed the contents with a grimace and then she set about packing.

* * *

When he returned Lily looked pale, her big eyes haunted, but she no longer looked as though she were sleepwalking.

'I'm all packed,' she said, nodding to the cases by the door.

'Your mum is expecting us?'

She nodded and stood up as he hefted her bags. As he approached the door with one under each arm she hurried to open it for him. 'The hotel rang her back for me. I should never have left Emmy with her.'

'Are you going to beat yourself up all the way? Just a question—it's fine, feel free.' He gestured towards his pocket. 'I brought my earphones just in case.'

The twitch of her lips *almost* constituted a smile. 'How long will it take…to get back?'

'It will seem a lot longer if you clock watch.'

She nodded, then clamped a hand to her mouth, covering a strangled sob. 'Sorry.'

The sound made something he chose not to name twist in his chest. 'You don't have to be sorry.' Ben felt a stab of shame that he had ever privately compared her maternal instincts with Signe's. 'I don't *know*, but from what people say kids can be ill one minute and bouncing around the next.'

Lily nodded.

A firm believer in straight talking, Ben was beginning to appreciate that there were times when it wasn't appropriate. 'But I suppose the medical establishment quite rightly tend to err on the side of caution when it comes to kids…'

She seized eagerly on his observation, nodding as she said, 'That's true. Mum only took Emmy to the doctor's because she just seemed a little off colour…and he said just to be on the safe side…so it's probably nothing, but I need to get back to her.'

The catch in her voice made the knot of unaccustomed emotion in his throat tighten. 'You will,' he promised huskily.

Lily took a deep breath and fought to damp down the rising sense of raw desperation, glad of the weight of the hand that had fallen on her shoulder.

She had never flown in anything nearly as luxurious as the private jet. Another time she might have enjoyed being waited on by the attentive staff, but as it was the time ticked by and the tension and fear inside her grew.

She wouldn't even have eaten had Ben not stood over and threatened to force-feed her if she didn't.

She pretended to be indignant, but she was actually rather touched that he was making such an effort to make her feel comfortable. Not that he personally brought her coffee or offered her a selection of glossy magazines—his staff did that. But for some reason when he left the cabin to talk to the pilot or take one of the numerous calls he received, it was harder to keep the dark fears in her head at bay.

Which was stupid; he had no magic power. What he did have was a presence. He radiated calm command. Normally it would probably have irritated her, but in this instance it made her feel as though everything would be all right.

Normally on a flight Ben either slept or worked. On this one he did neither—he just watched Lily. He'd been worried that she was going to fall apart but as the time passed he realised this wasn't going to happen. She was totally terrified—she didn't realise, but every thought in her head registered on her face—but Lily Gray, he realised, had an inner strength.

CHAPTER FIVE

As they emerged from the airport terminal, Ben took her elbow and led her to a waiting car. It was long and low with blacked-out windows and Ben spoke to the driver before sliding in beside her.

'Until I know what's happening I'd like to—'

'You don't want me there.'

She flicked an anxious look at his face. There was nothing to read in those strong lines and angles but she knew that she'd offended him. She seemed to have a knack at this and on this occasion she really didn't want to.

'You've been so kind.'

His chiselled jaw tightened. 'Kind is what a stranger is. I'm a father.' *Sounds good but what does it mean?* What did he actually know about being a father? Oh, arranging transport and second opinions he could do. That was the *easy* stuff. The other things…what if he was no good at them? What if he was a lousy father? His own father had probably meant well, but that hadn't stopped him failing miserably. Two parents waging their own silent war of attrition and he'd been the silent casualty.

'I didn't mean…' She looked at his shuttered profile

and, responding to an instinct she didn't pause to analyse, laid her small hand on his.

Ben looked from the small hand to her face. The muscles in his brown throat worked as he swallowed but his expression revealed nothing.

'You're a good mother.'

She blinked at the abrupt declaration before responding with a guilty flood of self-recrimination. 'I wasn't there... I should have been... Emmy needed me and I was with you—'

Ben felt the tortured guilt in the swimming green eyes that met his like a dull knife sliding between his ribs. He pressed a finger to her lips. 'You are now.'

She took a deep shuddering breath. 'Sorry.'

'When I was a kid I had a fall...fractured my skull.' He lifted a hand to the side of his head. 'There was internal bleeding and they had to operate to relieve the pressure. When my mother arrived—a week later—she was very concerned about the scars that might spoil my looks. Luckily the hair they'd shaved grew back. You *are* a good mother.'

A week...there were obviously scars that his hair did not hide. A good mother...who knew? *But at least I'm not a monster,* Lily thought soberly.

'So go be a good mum and I'll be around when you need me.' Earning his right to call himself a father.

'It's not that... Mum will be there on the ward, you see, and you... The explanations on top of everything else... I'm not trying to...exclude you.'

There was a long pause before he nodded. 'I have some calls to make. I'll have Martin...' he nodded towards the driver behind the glass screen '...drive around the block until you're finished.'

'But I might be a long time,' she protested.

He shrugged and handed her a mobile phone. 'Then you're a long time, but in case you need…anything.'

She looked at the phone.

'It has my number in it.'

Lily watched the man's lips move. Words came out, she could hear them, recognise them, but the words seemed disjointed, nothing he was saying made sense because this wasn't happening. She put down the full teacup, the contents cold, and turned her head to look through the glass partition where Emmy was sitting up in bed. She was wearing her favourite pyjamas and giggling as her grandmother pretended to search for the toy she clutched in her chubby little hands—it was one of her favourite games.

The emotion swelled in Lily's chest, the ache so intense that it drew a rasping sigh from her pale lips. This couldn't be happening. Emmy was too little, too… It was not fair!

Life isn't fair, said the unsympathetic voice in her head.

'Are there any questions you would like to ask me?'

Lily slowly turned her head; she felt weirdly frozen inside. 'Are you sure? Could there be a mistake? Results can get mixed up.' The magazines were always full of such stories. Hope flared and died in her eyes as the doctor, firm but sympathetic, put a hand on her shoulder.

'Your daughter is a very poorly little girl.'

Lily bit her lip, drawing blood but not noticing the metallic coppery taste on her tongue. 'But I'd have noticed.' *Should* have noticed. The guilt was there; it never went away. Her job as a mother was to protect…and she hadn't.

'This is not your fault.'

'Then whose fault is it?' she hissed, anger flaring then fizzling like cold ashes as he responded.

'Nobody's fault. The onset is notoriously insidious—the symptoms are often missed at this stage by professionals. Your GP did well to pick them up when he did, which puts us in a good position.'

Lily seized eagerly onto his words. 'It does?'

'At this stage ninety-five per cent of children go into remission following a bone-marrow transplant.'

Hope fluttered inside her skull. 'So bone marrow is a cure?'

'I don't want to raise your hopes.'

Too late, she thought, fighting a mixture of frustration and trepidation as he consulted the tablet he held.

A bunch of figures that spelt out her baby's future.

The man laid the tablet aside and removed his glasses. 'Though the number of bone-marrow donors have increased over recent years…'

Anticipating the *but*, Lily rushed into speech. 'She can have mine, can't she?' She laid her arm on the table and began to roll up her sleeve. 'Take what you like.'

'It doesn't work like that, I'm afraid,' the man said gently. 'I don't want to be negative, but the fact is that your daughter has an extremely rare blood group.'

Lily closed her eyes and released a low sigh as she finally realised where he was going. 'And I don't.'

'I have already discussed the subject of compatibility with your mother. She was unsure of the situation, Emily's father…paternal relatives. It is a relatively minor procedure for the donor though there is some discomfort involved.'

Lily surged to her feet feeling the first fluttering of real hope. 'Her father, he'll do it.'

The doctor gave a cautious smile and reminded gently, 'He'll need to be tested.'

She tilted her head again. 'He'll do it?' She heard the question in her own voice and from his questioning expression so did the doctor. 'He'll *want* to.'

And if he didn't?

She pushed the question away, she had to, because the other option… Her thoughts came up against the self-protective wall she had erected and bounced back.

Back on the ward, Lily gave an edited version of what the doctor had told her to her mother. They spoke softly because Emmy had fallen asleep, her thumb in her mouth. Looking at her made Lily's heart ache. That anyone so innocent should suffer…it seemed so *wrong.*

Elizabeth sat there in silence during Lily's halting delivery and then, with a hand pressed to her mouth, rushed from the room.

Lily found her a few moments later in the corridor, red-faced, but calm. 'This is the last thing you need. I'm sorry I didn't want Emmy to see… How are you, darling?' She held out her arms.

After a few moments Lily pulled free of the warm maternal embrace. 'I'm fine.' Empty was a better description, empty but for the sense of purpose that she focused on with tunnel-like determination.

'I have to leave, Mum.'

'But why? To go where?'

'I'll explain later, but I'll be back soon, I promise, and you have to go home for some sleep when I do.'

She kissed her mother's smooth cheek. 'You look exhausted.'

'It's not me I'm worried about.'

Lily's voice thickened. 'Have I said thank you for being there…for everything…?'

'What you don't seem to realise is that what you'd do for Emmy I would do for you. You're still my little girl.'

There were tears in Lily's eyes as she walked down the corridor. She dabbed at them impatiently and reminded herself there was hope. Outside it had begun to drizzle. Standing on the wet pavement, she fished out the phone Ben had given her and pressed the dial key. He picked up almost straight away.

'Ben, it's Lily, could you—?'

She stopped as a long limo drew up beside her, a window swished down and Ben, phone to his ear, leaned out.

Lily laughed. She hadn't really believed he was going to drive around the block.

'Need a lift?'

She nodded and the door swung open.

'Where to?' He studied her face and watched a single tear slide down her cheek, then another. He felt as if someone had reached into his chest and squeezed his heart. 'Oh, baby!' He reached for her and she drew back, a hand extended to ward him off.

'Do not touch me…don't!' she quivered out.

He stiffened.

'It's not you, it's me…if you touch me I'll start crying and I don't think I'll be able to stop!' she wailed.

He touched a teardrop on her cheek with his thumb. 'You're already crying.'

With a sob she flung herself at him. Ben looked

down at the fiery head pressed to his chest. After a pause his arms went around her and he let her cry herself out while he signalled the driver to carry on driving.

Embarrassed by her outburst and ashamed of her weakness, she finally pulled away. 'I must look terrible.'

'You look...' He stopped, an odd expression spreading across his face before he said abruptly, 'Fine. So...?'

He was prepared for the worst. He had been from the moment she had slid into the car emanating the sort of tension that did not say good news. And then she had started crying. He had never heard sobs like that before. They seemed to have been dragged from deep inside her. The sense of helplessness he had felt remained, a cold knot in his gut. He had dated beautiful women, women who were well groomed and elegant, and yet as he looked at Lily sitting there, her tear-stained face bare of all make-up, her hair a wild tangle, it struck him that he had never seen any woman look more beautiful.

'Sorry, I should have told you straight away.'

He took a deep breath. He was... No...*prepared* was a joke. Some things you couldn't be prepared for.

'She's very ill—'

She sniffed, visibly fighting for control, and Ben smothered a wave of protective concern that made him want to take her in his arms again. He was conscious that in her emotionally vulnerable state even small gestures could be misinterpreted, taken for something they were not.

He might be a bastard but he was at least an honest one. He'd never raised a woman's expectations in his life.

'Very ill, it's a...her blood. The doctor explained, but her best hope is a bone-marrow transplant.'

There was hope.

Listening, Ben knew how a man in a very long very black tunnel felt when a light appeared. He had a dozen questions but he closed his mouth, stifled his impatience and instead prompted gently.

'That's good.'

Her face told him there was a *but* coming.

'She has a very rare blood type and the chances of a donor being found in time are slim. Her main...only hope, really, is a compatible blood relative. I'm not compatible—' It still felt like a kind of failure that she wasn't able to be the one to save her child's life.

As soon as she mentioned the blood group he recognised the significance.

'But I am.'

Lily nodded. 'It seems likely. I don't really know about these things but I'm assuming if she didn't get my blood group she got yours? Though they wouldn't know for sure until they test you, but... I told him that you'd do it.' She felt his long fingers tighten on her forearm and looked down, not realising until that moment that he was holding her.

She looked up, wondering uneasily if she had taken too much for granted. Obviously she would do anything for her daughter, but Ben didn't even know her. He wanted to be involved, but she still couldn't shake the fear that deep down he might even resent her existence.

'I probably should have asked you first...'

He shook his head slowly from side to side. 'No, you should not have asked me. You'd do *anything* for Emmy, wouldn't you?'

'Of course, I'm her mother.'

'And I'm her father. So I would do anything for her

too.' *Anything...* His initial rush of emotions settled into deep relief.

'The fact that I can do something...' He spoke with more confidence as he realised he possessed the instincts he had feared were absent in his make-up. *'Anything...'* He dragged a hand across the surface of his gleaming dark hair and turned to the practicalities. 'I'll do it...when...how...?'

'The doctor said he'll see you in the morning. It's a relatively simple procedure. They can do it straight away. There's some discomfort,' she warned.

'Is it so hard for you to believe that I would endure the odd twinge for our daughter?'

She shook her head. 'Sorry. I suppose,' she admitted in a flash of shamed honesty, 'I feel a bit jealous. I wish *I* could be the one to save her. I know it's stupid and what matters is that she is saved.' She closed her eyes and said, 'But I wasn't even there for her... I wish I hadn't gone on that stupid holiday.'

'Emmy would still be ill.'

Her eyes opened and she nodded. 'Not rational, I know. I keep thinking about how I felt when I found out I was pregnant.' He saw an emotion he couldn't interpret flash in her eyes.

'You were scared?'

'I was stupid,' she retorted, closing her eyes to ease the ache behind them. 'You know, for weeks I was in denial. I just kept saying, like some sort of total idiot, it can't happen your first time, but of course it can and it did.' The words were out before she realised what she had said. Maybe he hadn't really been listening?

Slowly she opened her eyes and realised straight off that fate had not granted her a reprieve. Ben had heard and his lean face was frozen in a combination of shock and disbelief.

'First time...?' he prompted, in a low, dangerous voice while in his head another voice said, *No, not possible.*

It was simply not possible that the woman he had taken to bed that night had been...no, that was not possible.

'It doesn't matter.' Her little shrug was fuel to the flame of emotion that was burning him up. The guilt was eating him up from the inside out.

'My God, it's true—you were a virgin, weren't you? I was your first!' He looked at her as though she were a live grenade someone had dropped in his lap.

'Only...' *Oh, Lily what is wrong with you?* '...I've been pretty busy since.'

He closed his eyes. Lily couldn't take her eyes off the nerve that was clenching and unclenching beside his mouth.

'I don't believe it,' he groaned as he pushed one hand deep into his thick pelt of dark hair. He opened his eyes. 'A virgin?' He felt a fresh slug of guilt leavened with, if he was honest, a degree of arousal. It was a silly male possessive pleasure to know he'd been her first. 'You didn't say a word, and why me?'

'I thought you'd realise and, in case you haven't noticed, you are obscenely good-looking.' She'd hoped to lighten the mood but he didn't even crack a smile. If he looked like this now, she thought with a delicate little shudder, imagine how he'd look if she told him the full truth. Well, that was never going to happen. 'There's no need to make a big thing of it. I don't regret it. She's the most wonderful thing that has ever happened to me.

She was a beautiful baby and now…with what's going on, all that stuff doesn't matter now.'

Before he could respond the phone in her pocket began to vibrate—her own, not the one that Ben had given her. The sound of it was audible in the silence that had fallen.

Her hand was shaking as she reached into her bag then glanced at the screen. What she saw made her body stiffen. 'Sorry, it's the hospital. I have to check this.' She turned her face to the window to hide her expression as she replied. 'Yes, this is Lily Gray.'

She listened to the voice on the other end before giving a deep sigh of relief. 'That's marvellous, thank you so much, thank you.'

She turned, smiling, and responded to his arched brow with a shake of her head. 'Sorry, it's good news. It was the hospital to say there is a match on the register—a perfect match, they said, for Emmy. They are trying to contact him so it's possible you won't need to do anything.' She frowned. Ben was not listening. He was scrolling through his own phone—perhaps he didn't understand the significance of what she was saying. 'Apparently this person is someone who lives here in England. They warned me the odds were incredibly remote that they would find a match. If he agrees—'

Ben slid his phone back into his pocket. 'They've contacted him and he does agree.'

She looked at him, her blank look fading as he held up his phone and said softly, 'I've just been contacted.'

'You're on the bone-marrow register?'

'For a couple of years. A friend's wife needed a bone-marrow transplant so I got tested.'

'Did she get it?'

'Yes.'

His face told her nothing but she *knew,* she felt a cold clutch in her belly but ignored it. Emily was going to be all right. She'd make it all right.

'She didn't survive, did she…?' The impotent rage and ice-cold fear warring within her fought for an angry release. 'You can say it, you know.' Hearing the shrill note of irrational accusation in her voice, Lily took a steadying breath and dug into her reservoir of inner calm and found it empty.

'I'm *not* going to fall apart.' Falling apart was not an option. Emmy needed her; her mother needed her.

Studying her pale face and refusing to acknowledge the sharp stab of tenderness, he wondered if she thought saying it often enough would make it true.

'She'll be fine, you know, Lily.'

She nodded but couldn't meet his eyes. She was grateful that he was saying what she wanted to hear but she couldn't let herself believe it.

'So what do you think she'll make of me?'

It took her a moment to translate the emotion behind his question. Maybe because *insecurity* and fear were not words she associated with big, take-charge, in-control Ben.

Her tender heart ached 'She's two—she loves everyone.'

Ben gave a tight smile; he knew that love had to be earned. 'If I do it wrong, tell me.'

'There's no handbook, just wing it. It's what I've been doing for two years.' If genes had anything to do with it, Emmy would adore him—just like her mother.

CHAPTER SIX

AFTER A SELF-CONSCIOUS moment Lily disentangled her fingers from Ben's. She had no recollection of grabbing them.

'Could you drop me back at the hospital? I'm staying the night. Mum needs some sleep.'

It occurred to Ben that so did she, but, recognising that nothing he said would make her change her mind, he kept his opinion to himself.

'I'm seeing this Dr...?' Ben asked, when the limo drew up outside the glass-fronted hospital entrance.

'Sheridan,' she supplied. 'He's really nice.'

'I don't want nice,' he scorned. 'I want excellent.'

'I think he's both,' she said, finally releasing herself from the seat belt.

'Let's hope so.'

'The appointment is at nine. Apparently it shouldn't take long. Shall we meet up on the ward about ten? I'll introduce you to Emmy. You do know I'm grateful for this...'

He arched a sardonic brow. 'But...?'

She shook her head. 'No but, it's just... I think it might be better if we don't tell Emmy you're her dad straight away...' The words she had been silently rehearsing all the way emerged in a rush.

He looked at her with cynical ice-blue eyes. 'Better for who?' he asked bluntly.

Lily didn't react to the sarcasm. 'This is a confusing place for Emmy, everything that is happening, away from all her familiar things... Maybe it would be more appropriate later when she's feeling better...?'

Unable to maintain eye contact any longer with his accusing icy stare, she tipped her head and, reaching for the door handle, mumbled, 'Thanks,' as she stepped out of the car.

The anger inside him simmered. He watched her walk up the shallow flight of steps. It was transparently obvious to him she was letting him know that the door was open, probably hoping he'd walk through it.

He nodded to the driver, who restarted the engine just as she paused in front of the big glass revolving doors. From where he sat he could see her square her slender shoulders before she took that first step. A tiny but revealing gesture revealing an inner fragility he'd have preferred not to see. Then she was gone, but the image of her gathering her courage stayed with him.

Lily was standing the other side of the door when Ben was buzzed in. His arrival had the effect of a mild electric shock on her exhausted body.

He had lost the formal suit and was wearing a black leather jacket that hung open to reveal a contour-clinging top tucked into the belted waistline of black jeans that emphasised the length of his legs and hinted at the muscularity of his powerful thighs.

The overall effect was darkly dangerous and sinfully sexy without lessening his natural air of authority. Without turning her head to look Lily knew that the young nurse who appeared from the office was having her own appraising moment.

'You're here.' She bit her lip, stating the obvious. Their eyes clashed, but, other than the tension visible in the taut lines of his face, she struggled to read anything from his expression.

'So far so good, apparently. They're set to take the bone marrow this afternoon.' He had anticipated it would be more complicated, but all they needed apparently was a sterile environment and a local anaesthetic.

The smile that lit up her face made him uneasy.

'There is a long way to go,' he cautioned and saw her smile wobble. He stifled the urge to say something that would bring it back—there was no point being unrealistic.

If he'd had any doubts about the gravity of this situation, his daughter's doctor had dispelled them. The man had not made promises, but if he had Ben would have treated such reassurances with extreme scepticism.

The doctor in charge of his father's case had promised that he would be home by the weekend. Jack Warrender had never seen the weekend, dying of undiagnosed meningitis with only his teenage son at his bedside. His wife had been out of the room taking the inevitable important call.

When she had returned the only emotion to cross her features had been discomfort. 'You're too old to cry, Ben. Be a man... Have you seen my gloves anywhere?'

Ben had always believed until that day that, even though his mother put her career ahead of everything else, she did care for them. That belief died along with his father.

'Did he say anything?' his mother had asked Ben at

the funeral, as though the thought had just occurred to her. 'Your father? Before he died?'

'No,' Ben had lied. Not to save her, but because he didn't want to repeat the dying words his father had whispered...

'Marriage is a prison sentence, boy. A prison sentence. Don't do it.'

It remained the only advice his father had ever given him.

Lily closed her eyes briefly and let out a long sigh of relief. 'Good.' Sometimes words really weren't adequate.

It wasn't until she opened her eyes and followed the direction of his gaze that she realised she was literally wringing her hands.

She tucked them self-consciously behind her back while his attention switched to the young nurse who, with a pretty smile, explained the entire hand-washing and gowning-up routine to him.

'And if there's anything you need...' she touched the identity badge pinned to the lapel of her dress, her smile loosing several hundred watts of brilliance, and her manner became visibly more professional as she turned her head to include Lily '... I'll be in the office until one-thirty.'

Together they walked to Emmy's room in taut silence, both locked in their own thoughts.

'This is it.' She paused outside her daughter's room and turned to face him, tilting her head back. Crazily, even at a time like this, she felt the strong tug of attraction between them and was ashamed of her response to his raw maleness.

'Are you ready?'

The question produced a hard look and a long pause.

'You can change your mind if you want to.' Lily struggled to keep her voice free from inflection as she went to close the half-open door—this had to be his choice.

Ben leaned across her, his hand covering hers. 'I'm ready.'

Lily fought the weird compulsion to leave her hand where it was under his. Instead she pulled it free, put her head around the door, and nodded. Elizabeth, who was sitting at the bedside of the sleeping child, got to her feet.

Lily pushed away the mental image of her mum launching a verbal attack on Ben and crossed her fingers—she was doing that a lot lately. There had been little time for her mum to adjust to the knowledge that Ben was her granddaughter's father.

Lily hadn't known how to break it gently so she'd just blurted it out. 'Emmy's father is a probable match. It's Ben…Ben Warrender.'

After the initial stunned moments of shock, her mum had been angry and full of questions.

The former had been aimed at Ben, the latter at Lily.

'The choice was mine, Mum. I decided it would be better if he didn't know.'

'You mean you didn't even tell him you were pregnant?'

She had read the shocked condemnation in her mother's eyes, a look she'd imagined would be duplicated by strangers who got a whiff of the scandalous story. Lily didn't care what strangers thought of her, but it had hurt a lot to have her mum look at her with such disappointment.

'It wasn't that simple. There were...other factors.' Such as he'd split from his fiancée rather than give her a family.

'A man deserves to know he has a child, no matter what he's done.'

Lily had no idea what terrible things her mum had been imagining Ben had done. She'd chewed her lip in anguish. Having the disapproval shift her way had been, in many ways, easier. The last thing she needed was her mum being antagonistic to Ben.

'He really didn't do anything bad... I'm sorry I told you like this, Mum. You've had a shock. He has too.'

Elizabeth had shaken her head. 'I just don't understand why you did this, Lily. Surely your sister told you that you should—'

'Lara doesn't know either. Nobody knew.'

'You didn't even tell Lara? But you tell each other everything!'

Lily had shaken her head sadly. 'When we were children,' she'd said quietly. 'We don't confide the way we once did.' It saddened her that there was more distance than simple miles between them now. She missed the closeness.

Would they ever be close again?

She'd straightened her shoulders. This was her problem, not Lara's. 'The important thing is it looks like he is a match for Emmy and he's willing to be a donor.'

'Of course he's willing to be a donor, he's her father. If the man dared say no, you just give me five minutes with him.'

The continuing belligerence in her mother's attitude had dismayed Lily—she had enough eggshells to walk on without having to act a peacemaker between Ben and her mum.

'He won't. He's having further tests this morning and then he'll be... He wants to meet her.'

Her mum had sat down on a chair with a bump. 'I suppose he does,' she'd said faintly. She'd lifted a hand to her head. 'She looks like him, those eyes... Why on earth didn't I see it before?'

'I'm not Lara.' Her twin was the one that men looked at when she walked into a room. When they were together sometimes Lily felt invisible. It wasn't about looks, it was about confidence and personality and, yes...sensuality.

Her mother had frowned. 'What a strange thing to say, Lily. Whatever do you mean?' Her eyes had widened. 'Your sister didn't date him too?'

The mental image of her twin with Ben had been so real and the accompanying stab of shameful jealousy so strong that it had taken her a moment to react. 'No, of course not, I just meant you weren't looking for that connection—why would you be? I never dated men who were...like him.' There were no men like Ben.

What they had shared did not really qualify as a date... A dreamy expression had drifted briefly across her face as an image of the seafront café, the reflection of the lights on the water, had slid into her thoughts. It seemed like a lifetime ago. She'd shifted uncomfortably under the speculation in her mother's frowning regard.

'You won't make this hard...harder than it is,' she'd corrected, appealing, 'Will you, Mum?'

There had been a long pause and when her mum had finally shaken her head Lily had let out a long sigh of relief.

* * *

For a split second he really thought that Lily was going to block the door at the last minute, but then as she visibly straightened her slender shoulders she shifted to one side to allow him to enter the room before her.

Before he could do so Lily's mother emerged. The woman had always had a smile and a cheery word for him in the past, but now she walked past with her head disdainfully high. She blanked him completely until the last moment when she turned her head and tossed him a killer look that he presumed she reserved only for men who got her daughter pregnant.

He was a parent… Would it ever sink in?

Behind him he registered Lily's voice. The tone sounded urgent and pleading, but he tuned it out. All his focus was on that next step.

He took a deep breath, released it in a measured hiss and walked into the room.

In his life Ben had walked coolly into tough situations. Meetings where a false move or a show of weakness could lose him a fortune. He'd once got himself unexpectedly caught in the middle of a coup and found it exhilarating. Nerves were good. He used them; they gave him a vital edge.

He shoved his hands into his trouser pockets to hide the fact they were shaking. If only those people who said Ben Warrender had nerves of steel could see him now! As he walked into the room his body was bathed in a cold sweat. It was the hardest step he'd ever taken.

'She's asleep.'

He didn't react to the unnecessary information.

She'd seemed bigger somehow when he'd seen her at Warren Court, but now she was tiny, a baby really. She lay in a baby-sized bed, the sheet pulled up to her chin, one little hand clutching it tight. There were streaks on her face as though she'd been crying.

He gasped as he felt the emotion-tipped knife slide between his ribs straight into his heart. He had worried that he was incapable of loving anyone, even his own child… He'd been wrong. He knew now that he'd lay down his life in an instant for this sleeping angel.

Watching his face as he leaned forward and touched Emmy's cheek brought a massive aching lump of emotion to Lily's throat. The bleakness, the pain, the wonder… she recognised them all.

Then she saw the sheen of moisture in his eyes… *Sorry.* The word rattled around in her head and stayed there. What was the point in saying it? If the roles were reversed she'd never have forgiven him. The knowledge lay like a stone in her chest.

'I'll be outside,' she whispered huskily, turning her head so he didn't see her own tears as she left to give him some privacy.

It was some minutes later when he emerged. His handsome face was drawn and, though he had clearly been shaken by the emotional experience, he was in control now.

As her eyes meshed with his, without warning Lily's stomach clenched with desire that she stubbornly refused to acknowledge.

'She is a beautiful child.'

'I think so.'

'Will she sleep long, do you think?'

Lily nodded and explained, 'She had a bad night, so they gave her something. Last time it really knocked her out.'

'So you had a bad night too?' The shadows under her eyes made the answer obvious. She looked like a sepia copy of the radiant woman he had seen emerge from the sea. Still the most beautiful creature he had ever seen, but with a vulnerability that was programmed to arouse any man's protective instincts.

The response was not unique to him.

'Would you like a coffee?' she suggested tentatively. 'There's a machine in the visitors' lounge.' She tilted her head in the direction of a corridor to her right. 'It's just down here.'

He nodded.

The small lounge used by parents was empty. Lily walked across to the drinks dispenser, while Ben folded his long, lean length into one of the easy chairs that lined the wall. Stretching out, he crossed one booted foot over the other.

She was conscious of his eyes following her as she walked back.

'Black. I think it's coffee—it's hard to tell.' Her lips fluttered in a smile that didn't reach her eyes.

He looked at the paper cup for a moment before taking it and grimaced, but didn't comment as he lifted it to his lips.

'Sorry about Mum—she's still in shock.'

His lashes lifted off his chiselled cheekbones. 'There's a lot of it about.'

Lily lifted her chin a defiant notch. 'I did what I thought was right at the time.' Not long ago she had had no doubts that her choice was the right one. Now…she thought again of his face, the pain and regret she had seen in his eyes.

She pushed away the guilt, but it resisted. There was no escaping it—she'd been wrong.

'And there's no going back. This is the way it is.' She wished she could feel as hard and practical as she sounded.

'We should talk.' Because the world carried on, life carried on. Even when just down the corridor the baby he had fathered fought for her life. 'The lawyers have drawn up a trust fund for your approval.' A spasm of self-loathing crossed his face and he squeezed his eyes shut and shook his head. 'God, that must sound incredibly crass of me, talking about money when—'

'No!' she cut in. 'You're talking about Emmy's future...you believe she has one.' She gave him a watery smile of gratitude and Ben felt something in his chest tighten.

He studied her face. 'But maybe this can wait till later?'

Lily nodded. 'Mum is heading back home to pick up some things. Everything happened in such a rush, she's worn the things she has on for two days straight, and Emmy has forgotten Timmy. Her teddy bear,' she explained, catching his look. 'I should get back to relieve her.' She glanced at the clock on the wall above the doorframe just as a couple came in. She had seen them before. The woman was weeping on the shoulder of her husband, whose face was grey and strained.

The stab of sheer visceral fear made Lily oblivious to the hot liquid she spilled down her front. She stood blinking as the empty cup was prised from her hand.

'Come on.' There was no resistance in her trembling body as Ben urged her from the room. As he reached the door his glance connected with the husband of the weeping woman. The level of understanding in that look brought the situation sharply into focus...he might lose a daughter he had not known he had.

Lily looked at the tissue extended to her and shook her head, clinging to her self-control with the grim determination of a drowning man grabbing a lifeline. 'It's fine...' She dug her teeth down hard into her trembling lower lip. 'I'm not going to cry.'

'Maybe you should,' Ben roughed out, fighting off the protective feelings her delicacy and distress had shaken loose inside him. It mingled with the ever-present lust—the combination was one short teeth-grinding step from insanity. 'There's nothing wrong with letting go.' Good advice, he told himself, thinking of the anger he had nursed towards Lily, now recognising it for what it was—a self-indulgence for which he didn't have the time or energy to spare. 'It would be some sort of outlet,' he told her evenly. 'You're carrying around a lot of stress.'

The comment brought her chin up with an angry jerk. Her green eyes blazed. 'My daughter, my beautiful baby daughter who has never done anything to anyone, never had a mean thought in her life, is fighting for her life. Stress? Yes, I suppose you could say that!' She stopped, her chest heaving, and pressed a hand to her mouth. 'Sorry, I... Sorry, it's not your fault—' She gritted her teeth over a gulping sob.

He had reared back as though struck when she'd begun to yell, but when the first tear fell his anger had melted away. 'It's nobody's fault, Lily.'

He touched her shoulder and with a lost little cry that he felt at a cellular level she pressed her face into his chest. 'I should have known,' she wailed. A moment later she was straightening up, wiping her face with the backs of both hands and shaking her head. 'I am so sorry. You don't want to hear this.'

'This is my child too.' Head back, he dragged a hand through his hair, missing her wince. 'This place...' His blue eyes brushed her face. 'I'm not keen on hospitals. I could do with some fresh air. So could you.'

If she got any paler she could have been taken for a ghost. *Except ghosts didn't have hair like fire.* His eyes followed the sweep of the glorious curls over her slender shoulders and down her back. The inevitable warmth in his belly, the hot charge that zigzagged through his body, was mingled with a less explicable tenderness— she looked so damn fragile it hurt.

He couldn't explain it. God knew he was no white knight, but maybe there was a part of him that was pre-programmed to respond to that vulnerability.

Lily, who hadn't even looked in a mirror for two days, was suddenly conscious of how awful she must look. The coffee stains added the finishing touch.

'I need to get back—'

'Five minutes.'

He didn't wait for her response, just put a hand in the middle of her back and started walking. Lily didn't have the strength to resist and maybe fresh air would be good.

She didn't know how he did it. The hospital was several vast old buildings plus new additions all linked by a series of glass connecting corridors, yet he didn't once glance at the overhead signs as he led them through the maze of corridors unerringly to a side door that opened to the outside world.

Lily closed her eyes and took several deep breaths.

Like someone in a trance, she stood there staring at the skyline until the sound of an ambulance siren made her start. They were in the visitors' car park. It was quiet and empty at the moment, but soon would begin to fill.

She glanced over her shoulder at the hospital building. 'I should go back in.'

'You should go to bed, but I know you won't.' It was hard to maintain his anger. Part of him had wanted to find fault, but, whatever else she was, Lily was obviously a devoted mother.

Her lips ghosted a faint smile as she lifted her face to him. She brushed the wisps of gold red hair from her face, leaving one free, which Ben fought a sudden urge to tuck behind her ear.

'There will be plenty of time to sleep afterwards...' As he watched a stricken expression spread across her face she rushed into explanatory speech. 'I didn't mean it like that...she will be all right, won't she?' She shook her head and murmured a soft, almost inaudible, 'Sorry.'

'For what?'

'For asking you to tell me it will be all right.' She lifted her chin; she knew it would be a massive mistake to fall into the habit of thinking they were a team. 'You don't know... I don't know... We have to put our reliance in medical science and blind luck.'

'Don't knock luck and aren't you forgetting a little girl's fighting spirit?'

'I wish I could do it for her...'

'I know.'

On the point of leaning into him, she pulled back. 'I should go back...' Behind her the door was caught by a gust of wind and slammed, rattling the glass. She turned her head at the sound and wondered how long it would take to find her way back to the ward.

'Where are you staying?'

She turned her head and looked at him, a frown of incomprehension forming between her feathery brows. 'Staying?' she echoed.

'Sleeping.'

'Oh, they recommended a nice B & B near the hospital.' Her arm lifted in a vague directional gesture. 'Mum booked us in there. She's dropping off my bag on her way home, I think.'

His mouth thinned into a critical line. 'That hardly seems ideal.'

'This situation is not ideal!' she flared bitterly, then tacked on a weary, 'Sorry.' Immediately regretting venting her anger and frustration at him—she didn't blame him, he was just there.

Were there couples whose relationships were casualties of a situation like this? she wondered. Were there bleak statistics out there to confirm it? Well, one thing they couldn't become was a statistic. They weren't a couple; they were already apart.

Suddenly very cold, she gave a shiver.

'Do you want to go in?'

She gave an absent nod, tucking her hair behind her ears as she tilted her head to look up at him. 'They are very good here. They try their best. The unit has a purpose-built apartment block for parents and families, but it's vastly oversubscribed and pretty much on a first-come-first-served basis. Anyway I actually prefer to sleep in the chair by Emmy at the moment—just in case...' She gulped, her eyes falling from his, but not before he had seen the terror she struggled to ignore.

He fought against the instinct to offer her comfort. 'I understand.'

Bracing her shoulders, she exhaled a gusty sigh. Her voice no longer quivered and was firm with conviction as she said, 'She'll be all right. I know she will. It was just seeing that couple—they were so happy yesterday...' She shook her head as if to shake away the scene in the day room. 'It was a good idea to get some fresh air.'

'It helps. I hate being inside hospitals.'

'Do you hate hospitals because of your accident?' She encountered his blank expression and touched her own head.

'Oh, that.' He shrugged. 'No one *likes* hospitals.'

Suddenly Lily felt very angry, remembering what he'd told her about his mother. 'I just don't get... How *could* she?'

Ben shook his head.

'She was your mother. How *could* she leave you alone? Was your father there?'

'He was in the middle of a project or affair, maybe both. He was good at multitasking, but I got the best medical care money could buy.' Her empathy was beginning to make him uncomfortable. He did not think of himself as an object of pity. 'This is the part where I normally bring out the violins.' He cocked his head to his shoulder and pretended to play a violin.

'It's not funny!' Maybe making a joke of it was his way of coping?

'My grandfather came,' he said, hoping this would stop her flow of indignation.

'Was that when they sent you to live with him?'

Ben shook his head, exasperated by her persistence. 'No, that was a couple of years later and I sent myself.'

'Sent?'

'I packed my bags and told them I was going, end of story.'

Her emerald eyes widened in astonishment. 'And they let you?'

'I didn't ask permission and I imagine they were secretly relieved. So was I when my grandfather let me stay.'

'Have you told him yet, your grandfather, about Emmy?' She took his expression as a no. 'I'll give Mum a ring and ask her not to tell him before you've had a chance to speak to him. You can't let him hear something like this from a stranger. He's old.'

'Old and as tough as old boots,' Ben retorted, no inflection in his voice.

'Maybe,' she conceded. 'But at his age something like flu can take a long time to get over.'

The comment slid through his defences. 'He had flu?'

'You didn't know?' She was startled.

Ben compressed his lips, his jaw hard as he turned and curved his hands around the cold metal rail he had been leaning against before admitting, 'We had a ten-minute conversation last week. I hadn't been home... well, since the last time and he threw me out.'

'I assumed you'd had a falling out...'

Ben opened his mouth to tell her that it was none of her business and instead found himself responding to her probing with an explanation.

'My efforts to update the estate did not go down well. He accused me of being heartless and avaricious.' An accusation that had left a bitter taste in his mouth because Ben was pretty sure that, even though he'd never mentioned it to his grandfather, the old man knew about the money Ben had surreptitiously sunk into various projects on the estate. Unless he thought the aged machinery in the saw mill renewed itself? 'It appears he thinks forward planning involves selling off a painting or a piece of land to settle debts.'

Lily felt a stab of sympathy for both men. 'I suppose it's hard for someone like your grandfather to relinquish control...young lion, old lion type of thing...?' she suggested tentatively. 'People need to feel needed.'

'There's just no talking to the man!' The explosive complaint left his lips before he could censor it. He shrugged, moderating his tone as he added, 'But I will tell him about Emily Rose.'

Hopefully the shock would not see him off, he thought grimly. Would it heal any rifts? The jury was still out on that one.

'When?'

'Next weekend,' he decided, estimating the time the round trip would take him by helicopter as he unzipped his leather jacket. 'The next time Elizabeth wants to go back to Warren Court let me know—you can use the chopper. It's at her disposal any time she wants it.'

Lily blinked at the generous offer.

'And you, of course.'

Lily, who had no plan to go anywhere, nodded then frowned as he removed his jacket. Underneath he wore a thin long-sleeved top. 'What are you doing?'

In response he took hold of the hem of the cashmere top.

Panic slid through her. It turned out to be justified because a moment later he was standing there naked from the waist up, revealing his muscle-ridged golden torso to anyone who might be passing.

Only there was no one in the car park but her. Her own private striptease.

She had no control over the movement of her wide eyes as they made a covetous sweep from his broad, powerful shoulder to his ribbed belly. The warmth that began in the pit of her belly spread outwards until she was burning and hot all over. A sound that was half moan, half protest left her mouth as she struggled to tear her gaze free. He had a body like a classical statue.

'Well, come on, I'm getting cold.' He sounded impatient.

She looked at the top he held out to her and closed her mouth with an audible snap.

'Do you really want to spend the rest of the day looking like that?'

Lily followed the direction of his gaze downwards, registering for the first time the coffee stains all down her front. There were some splashes on her slim-legged trousers but her top was totally ruined. She patted ineffectually at the still-damp stains, stopping as she recognised it was a lost cause—she barely even remembered spilling the coffee. What had it been—five, ten minutes ago...? It felt as though it had happened in another life!

She looked at the fabric fluttering slightly as a breeze caught it and her brain belatedly translated the gesture—he was offering her his top.

'Thanks, but I couldn't possibly—'

'There isn't a hidden catch.'

'You need it!' she declared, shaking her head and not delving too deeply into why she was so desperate to think of an excuse not to put the garment, still warm from his skin, on her bare flesh.

'I have a jacket. It may not be your colour, Lily, but it is a practical solution.'

Lily sighed and gave in, grumbling, 'What did you say about your grandfather? It's his way or no way?' She saw his startled expression before she turned around and, presenting her back to him, whipped her soiled top off, gasping a little as the cool air touched her skin.

His top settled against her skin, still warm from his body. It carried his scent mingled with expensive male fragrance or maybe soap. She felt a stab of guilt as her stomach muscles reacted to the intimacy of the shared body heat.

What sort of mother was she, distracted by sex at a moment like this?

She tugged her hair loose from the top and as she turned back Ben was zipping his jacket up, giving Lily a brief glimpse of his golden toned skin against the dark leather.

She knew that the image was going to stay with her.

He stood looking at her, his head a little to one side. 'It looks better on you than it does on me.'

Blatantly not true. The garment, which was snug-fitting on him, was loose on her and hung baggily down almost to her knees. Lily despised her stomach-fluttering response to his compliment. And the fluttering got considerably worse when, without explanation, he stepped forward and began to competently roll first one sleeve and then the other up to her elbow level. His dark head was close enough for her to smell his shampoo as he performed the task.

Lily fought the impulse to lean into him. They shared a child but they were not a couple. She needed to remember that. She took a hasty, and not very elegant, step backwards.

'Thanks.'

Without another word she vanished through the door. He picked up the soiled top she had dropped on the floor and, before he pushed it into the conveniently placed waste bin, found himself yielding to the impulse to lift it to his face.

His nostrils flared in response to the lemony scent it carried. He needed to be careful. Lily was vulnerable, and she was the sexiest, most sensual creature alive. It would be easy to forget that the closeness they were experiencing was temporary. Yet it was the closest he had ever been to a woman.

And what does that say about you, Ben?

It said he had the good sense to keep clear of close relationships. Having witnessed firsthand the war that had passed for his parents' marriage, Ben had decided early on that he was never going to walk into a relationship he wasn't able to walk out of.

But he wouldn't walk away from his daughter.

CHAPTER SEVEN

BEN HATED THIS awful white box of a room. He hated hospitals, he hated relying on medical science, he hated feeling helpless, useless... Ben surged to his feet, wincing as his chair scraped noisily on the floor.

In her cot Emmy continued to sleep, although she stirred a little and so did Lily in her chair. Quietly he made his way to the door and, holding his breath, closed it carefully behind him. He turned and found Elizabeth Gray standing there watching him.

Since he had made his bone-marrow donation her attitude had thawed. There was just a thin layer of frost now when she spoke to him.

Ben didn't blame her.

'They're asleep. I was just going to get some fresh air.'

'Lily said you reminded her of a tiger in a cage.'

'Did she? I don't really like hospitals. Can I get you anything? Coffee?'

Ben took her rejection philosophically and was about to move away when her voice made him turn back.

'Can I ask you something that I've always been curious about?'

'Sure you can ask. I can't guarantee I'll answer.'

Having braced himself to defend behaviour that, from any loving parent's point of view, was indefensible her actual question took him by surprise.

'Your parents had what most people would call an unhappy marriage.'

'That's putting it politely. Others would call it hell.'

'I always wondered, why did they stay together? They weren't religious or—?'

Ben gave a dry laugh. It was a question he had asked himself on more than one occasion. 'Honestly, I don't have a clue. They both threatened it over the years, but neither carried through... Maybe in some twisted way, for them at least, the marriage worked...' he speculated with a mystified shake of his head '...or it could be that they were just too stubborn to admit they'd made a mistake.'

Elizabeth nodded. 'Some people should not be together.'

'Marriage is a leap in the dark,' he countered cynically.

'What about your investments? Don't they involve the same thing?' she teased gently.

He angled a narrow-eyed look at her face. 'Are you trying to get in my head, Mrs Gray?'

She smiled. 'Call me Elizabeth.'

'Risks are easy when you're only dealing with money, Elizabeth.'

'You know, I think I might have that coffee, Ben.'

He sprinted for the lift, silently cursing the estate agent who'd made him late. He glanced at his watch—had he missed the doctor's round?

It was all the estate agent's fault. The guy had been

creating problems where there were none, as far as Ben was concerned. He had zero interest in getting the best deal or calling anyone's bluff. If the vendors wanted more money, they could have it.

In the end, he'd had to spell it out.

'Give them a blank cheque. I don't give a damn, so long as I have the keys for tomorrow.'

The guy had looked at him as though he was insane.

'Blank cheque?' he'd echoed, sounding scandalised by the suggestion.

Ben had silenced him with a look.

This morning the guy had been sitting with his commission cheque in his hot hand, telling Ben that it had been a pleasure doing business with him and apologising profusely for having one last paper for him to sign.

Walking down the long corridor that led to the specialist unit, he passed a couple he recognised and nodded before continuing on. His stab of sympathy was mingled with a feeling of relief. It was weird, but you quickly got to know when people had had bad news, simply from their body language.

Buzzed onto the ward, he did not hurry the hygiene rules. The strict measures to protect the vulnerable child from infection had become second nature to him over the past couple of weeks. Shrugging on the gown, he almost collided with the two figures standing outside Emmy's room.

Ben felt as if someone had reached into his chest; the icy fingers tightened around his heart as the implications of what he was seeing hit him. He froze as Lily, oblivious to his presence, her head on her mother's shoulder, continued to weep uncontrollably.

For the past couple of weeks she had kept a constant

vigil at Emmy's bedside, refusing a bed when one came up in the purpose-built block that housed parents of children who arrived at the specialist centre from all over the country. It was the best; Ben had made it his business to find out. During that time her cheerful, positive façade had stayed firmly in place. On the couple of occasions it had slipped and she'd needed to vent, he had been philosophical about taking the flak—at least he was good for something and there was precious little else he could do.

He had suffered moments of black doubt, but not Lily. There had never been any *if,* it had always been *when* Emily Rose got better.

While the doctors had been upbeat about the outcome, apparently it was rare for a parent to be a full match but he was. They had warned that compatibility, even full compatibility, did not guarantee success. They spoke a lot about multiple factors affecting the outcome.

Had Lily heard them? Or had she, as he suspected, tuned out anything she couldn't cope with? The latter, he suspected. It had been obvious from the outset that she was in denial and intended to stay that way.

Ben had tried not to think how she would react if the worst happened...now he knew. The sound of her sobs tore at him, as did his sense of total, utter helplessness.

Less than three weeks ago he hadn't known he had a child. He hadn't known what he'd feel; not feeling anything had been his biggest fear. Yet when he had walked into the room and seen the tiny, terrifyingly frail figure lying asleep in the white hospital bed, her eyelashes fanned out across cheeks that might have once been rosy but were now pale as milk, emotions he had not known existed, feelings he hadn't known he was capable of, had welled up in his chest. So strong he'd felt as if he were drowning.

He had hoped, he had prayed that he could learn to love his child, to prove himself worthy, but there was no learning involved. It was as genetically pre-programmed as breathing.

These were feelings that he'd never have known. Fear that he was as selfish and cold as his mother, or as un-interested as his father, would have kept him from ex-periencing them if Lily hadn't fallen pregnant.

Their two-year-old had shown more guts than he had! He should have thanked Lily instead of blaming her. Whichever way you looked at it, half the respon-sibility and blame was his. Was it any wonder she had been and still was wary of his attempts to be part of Emmy's life? It was not a right, it was a privilege and one that Ben had set out to prove himself worthy of.

Too late. He closed his eyes, drawing in a deep shud-dering breath, seeing a stream of images. They hurt but he prized each one. For the past two weeks, since Emily Rose had been infused with his cells, he had seen her every day. He had felt despair and anger as he'd watched her suffer, helpless to do a thing about it. His face-to-face contact was limited to a few short periods when Lily ate or showered; how she coped remained a mystery to him.

She smiled but her eyes held a haunted look that no amount of optimism could disguise. And, in unguarded moments, a sense of helplessness and despair he rec-ognised all too well.

There were times when, to vent his anger or frus-tration, he wanted to hit something. Instead Ben chan-nelled his energies to more practical things.

A firm believer that knowledge was power, and for once in his life he felt he had precious little of that, Ben read up on the disease so that he had a better understanding of the information the medical staff disclosed.

He set himself achievable goals. Sometimes they seemed pathetically small, like making Emmy laugh twice a day. He was not Daddy—it was much too soon—so he was the funny man. Encouraging her to eat at least two mouthfuls of everything on her meal plate. And making sure that when the time came they wouldn't find themselves in the same situation as other families—whose discharge had been delayed because they lived outside the area that allowed quick access should an emergency arise—hence his meeting with the estate agent.

When did I start thinking of us as a family?

The solution to the last problem had been simple: buy a suitable house. Today he'd ticked that off his list, but his quiet sense of satisfaction vanished the moment he saw Lily's tears. He felt the implication like a fist landing with the force of a sledgehammer in his solar plexus. He stood frozen, immobilised by the emotions that broke free inside him.

As she drew back from her mum's embrace a movement in the periphery of her vision made Lily turn her head. Ben was standing there raking a hand through his dark hair that over the last couple of weeks had grown longer, curling crisply against his collar. Through the loose white gown, that they all wore on the ward, she could see one of the brightly coloured ties he had taken to wearing every day.

The sight of him revealing the day's fashion faux

pas with a magician-like flourish to Emmy never failed
to make Lily's throat tighten. Today it made her howl.

His face contorted as he held out his arms. 'I am
so, so sorry.'

Her normal mantra of *Don't rely on him, he might not
be here tomorrow* failed. Today she was too emotional,
too giddy with relief to show the normal level of caution.
Instead, crying out his name, she flew into his arms.

Enfolded in his strength, her head against his chest,
it took her a few moments to realise what he was saying as he stroked her hair... 'Sorry...sorry.'

She pulled back, catching his big hand between the
two of hers as she looked up into his face shaking her
head. 'No...no... I'm crying because I'm happy.' She
sniffed, loosening his hand and pressing both of hers
to her face.

'Happy?'

Her hands fell away; her lovely eyes, red-rimmed
and bloodshot from many sleepless nights, glowed as
though lit from within.

'It's taken. Emmy is going to be all right—the transplant has taken. You know the last results were—' she
lifted her hands and sketched ironic inverted commas
in the air '—promising? Well, the latest results are back
and they are conclusive—the transplant has taken.'

Ben didn't do anything, he just stood there staring
at her, much the way she had done when the doctor had
taken her to his office to break the good news. Barely
aware of what she was doing, she grabbed one of his
hands and, lifting it, pressed her cheek to his palm before pressing a kiss to it.

Laughing, she barely registered his expression as she
turned and hugged her mother before swinging back

to Ben. 'It's taken, Ben, it's really taken.' Her voice cracked and broke with emotion.

Ben watched the tears spill from her eyes. His entire body felt as a frozen extremity did when the circulation returned…feeling had burned away the protective layer that had enabled him to function, stripping his emotions bare. With a painful stab of self-awareness he knew there would be no going back. A man could walk around with a void inside him once he recognised it for what it was—fear.

Lily was laughing and crying, squeezing his hand again. He struggled to respond, to match her bubbling happiness.

'I thought—'

'Sorry, I know.' She took a deep steadying breath. 'I have to say thank you. If it wasn't for you Emmy might not be here. You've been kind even when I… I will never forget what you did.'

Ben pulled his hand away, suddenly annoyed. 'I didn't do it for that. I don't want your gratitude.'

If she asked him what he did want, what would he say?

She didn't ask him, she just looked at him, clearly puzzled by his reaction, so he asked himself. What did he want?

His eyes widened as the answer surprised him.

Lily tentatively touched his arm. 'Are you all right?' Well, that was what she'd intended to say, but she wasn't sure whether it all came out because quite suddenly her knees went, there was a loud buzzing in her head and the floor came up to meet her.

Ben stepped forward and caught her before she hit the ground. Grunting softly, he hefted her higher into his arms. 'Could we have a doctor here?' Looking down at the pale face of the woman in his arms, he felt emotions he had spent weeks struggling not to acknowledge break free. 'The place is full of bloody doctors, so where are they when you need one?'

'Is she breathing?' They all had their breaking point and this was obviously Elizabeth's. 'She's not breathing.'

'She is,' he assured her. 'She's just fainted. Exhausted probably.'

'Thank God, thank God, I knew this would happen!' Maternal concern found release in a shrill string of loving criticism as Elizabeth patted her unconscious daughter's head. 'I knew it! You have no idea how stubborn she can be! She just can't accept help, it's always *I don't want to be a bother...* Bother? She's my little girl. I want to help. I need to help.'

Her words resonated. *I need to help.* He totally understood the sentiment. It remained one that he was unable to articulate. After he had done his part, he could have walked away. He knew that Lily had expected him to. She probably would have preferred him to walk away.

His jaw muscles locked tight as he looked down at this fiercely independent woman, half her face hidden in his shoulder. He struggled to poke his anger into life but instead experienced an overwhelming surge of protectiveness. It was primal and illogical, a throwback to hunter-gatherer days.

It was love.

They were right. Love did set you free. In his case the prison bars had been of his own making.

'She'll be fine, Elizabeth, just let...' Blocked in a

corner, he tried to ease past the woman, calling out, 'In here, she fainted!' Relieved to finally see assistance in the form of a nurse and a doctor, he reluctantly passed Lily onto the trolley that arrived.

As a child she had always been cynically sceptical of those scenes in films when the swooning heroine lifted a hand to her head and said in a faltering voice, *'Where am I?'*

As she opened her eyes and mumbled, 'Did I faint?' she felt some sympathy for those heroines.

'Yes.'

Her eyes flew wide at the sound of his voice. Ben, she discovered, was standing beside the bed she lay on looking stern and—she gave her head a tiny shake—he was wearing what she thought of as his closed look.

'Well, I suppose I did it in the right place,' she said, struggling to pull herself upright, only to find her progress hindered by a large hand in the middle of her chest. 'Will you stop that? I have to—'

'You have to stay there and sit up gradually. Then you will drink this vile cup of tea the kind nurse made you, while I will go and reassure your mother that you are all right. Then I am taking you back home, where you will sleep.'

Out of the list Lily could see herself doing one: the cup of tea sounded good.

'I'm—'

'Let me guess, fine?' he drawled, sounding bored.

'Well, I am.' She directed a pointed look at his hand planted on the middle of her chest. 'But I won't be if I can't breathe.'

The pressure immediately lessened, which did not

help the breathless feeling, suggesting it had more to do with than his proximity. She pressed her eyelids closed and breathed in the scent of his skin. Blindfolded, she could find him in a room of a hundred people; it was terrifying how fine-tuned all her senses were to him.

'Can I get up now?' *Unaided, Lily,* she reminded herself. Despite all her best intentions, she had leaned on him a lot during the last couple of weeks, and he'd been there. She was under no illusion, despite his deeply developed sense of duty, now that Emmy was out of danger how much contact he would want.

Access was the least she owed him; it was a debt she could not begin to pay. During the last weeks of uncertainty, her entire focus had been on her daughter's... their daughter's recovery. Lily had not even begun to think about what happened next, once Emmy was out of danger.

'Slowly.'

She did so, swinging her legs over the side of the bed. They were in a curtained cubicle in an empty bay of beds. As she got up he pulled aside the curtain with a swish of fabric.

'You all right?'

She lowered the hand she had lifted to her head. 'Fine,' she lied, fighting a wave of nausea.

'Drink the tea.' He wheeled the trolley closer and pointed at it.

'Is that an order?' His attitude made her want to grind her teeth and do the exact opposite, but she was awfully thirsty so it probably wasn't worth making a fuss.

'Don't shoot the messenger.'

His ironic comment brought her eyes to his face, seeing for the first time the lines of strain etched around his spectacular eyes. Over the last couple of weeks she had rarely given much thought to how he was feeling.

'This stoic stuff is admirable, to a point,' he continued, 'and then it just gets irritating. I know it goes against the grain for you to agree with anything I say and you have established the fact that my opinion counts for nothing. But none of those points are my idea. They are the doctor's orders. Emily Rose,' he said, enjoying giving her her full title, 'is asleep. And you will be of little use to her if you end up as a patient here yourself.'

'All right.'

His brows lifted at the ready capitulation. 'Common sense? Will wonders never cease?'

She acknowledged the rueful comment with a twitch of her nose and admitted, 'I know I need sleep, but I haven't been able to switch off for weeks. I think I've forgotten how.'

She gave a yawn and a stretch and, his eyes on the smooth section of midriff it revealed, he found himself thinking of several interesting methods of helping her *switch off*... He on the other hand felt very switched on!

She lowered her arms, but the damage was done; all he could think about was kissing a path up the soft curve of her belly...or down and—

'Besides, I couldn't bear for her to wake up and be alone.'

The plaintive admission made him feel like a total bastard, when all he could think about was getting her clothes off.

'She's not going to be alone when she wakes up,' he soothed, the colour scoring his cheekbones the only remaining evidence of the frustration that burned in his veins. 'Your mother will be there and the nurses who, let's face it, she has managed to wrap around her little finger.'

Lily grinned then yawned again, her hand patting her mouth. If this didn't stop soon she'd dislocate her jaw. 'She really is a charmer, isn't she?' she agreed with pride. 'You're right.'

'Now that hardly hurt at all, did it?'

She shot him a look. 'I do need some sleep. Could you give me a lift to the B & B?' Did that sound pushy? 'Or if you're busy I could get a cab. Oh, could you ask Mum for the room card?' Though Lily had only been to the small B & B once or twice, her mum had been sleeping there—except on the couple of occasions she had taken advantage of Ben's offer of his helicopter and flown back home.

On the last occasion she had come back that same evening admitting that she could get very used to that form of transport. Then she had broken the news to Lily that her secret was no longer a secret.

News travelled fast in a small rural community and everyone now knew the identity of Emmy's father.

Lily hadn't really expected the news to spread so quickly. She had half anticipated that Ben's grandfather might have wanted to bury the truth but he hadn't and Lily found, rather to her own surprise, that she was not particularly concerned.

The only person she hadn't wanted to know was Ben and now that he did, other people gossiping didn't really matter to her.

'Not walk?' he mocked.

'Actually I could, couldn't I?' She realised, missing the irony totally, the small B & B where her mum had taken a room was literally just round the corner from the hospital.

The initial idea had been for them to take turns sleeping there, but Lily had found it much less stressful to sleep in a chair by her daughter's bed.

He looked at her for a moment and shook his head. 'No, you couldn't. I will take you, though obviously I will expect petrol money.'

The comment drew a reluctant smile from Lily. It was so much easier to smile now that the crushing weight of fear she hadn't even been conscious of carrying had been lifted. It was there but no longer oppressive. It wouldn't be gone until they were home.

'Thank you.' She took a sip of the tea and grimaced before calling after him. 'It's incredible, isn't it?'

Framed in the open doorway, he turned. She was sitting there on the bed cross-legged, her face framed by wild curls. Smiling, she looked too young to be a mother. The effort of not crossing the room and pulling her under him on the bed was hard enough to bring beads of sweat to his upper lip.

She was incredible, so sweet and brave. Of course, she was also stubborn enough to drive a man insane, but he imagined most men would consider it a privilege.

'It is, yes.'

Until he spoke Lily hadn't been aware that she was holding her breath. As he vanished she released it, conscious of a gnawing sense of anticlimax. Had she imagined the tension in the air, the heavy throb of sexual awareness…?

Ten minutes later, her blood pressure had been checked and she had been discharged by a junior doctor who, in

Ben's opinion, had a hell of a lot to learn about professional distance. Now they made their way to the main entrance.

Lily read out loud the sign above the space near the main entrance where Ben had parked his long sleek silver car.

'Reserved for the Chief Administrative Officer.'

'What can I say? I'm a rebel.' Torn between irritation and amusement, because she seemed genuinely outraged at the rule infringement, he made a placatory gesture. 'Trust me, you're more likely to see a flock of pigs fly past than see an administrator at work on a Saturday.'

Lily had forgotten it was the weekend, slightly alarming, but she wouldn't let it go without making her point. 'What would happen if we all went around breaking the rules?'

'You think a bit of illegal parking is going to trigger the downfall of society?'

She gave a sudden grin. 'No, but it's fun winding you up.'

'You little—!'

Heart pounding, she waited, but before Ben reached her a man in a porter's uniform appeared, almost hidden behind the enormous elaborate flower arrangement he carried.

'Miss Gray?'

Lily nodded, then, realising he couldn't see her, said, 'Yes?'

'I'm on the front desk today, thought I saw you leaving.' A head appeared around the side and she recognised one of the porters who had taken Emmy down to the X-ray department a few times. 'This arrived for you.'

'I'll take that.' Ben took the package by the handle of the massive wicker basket that the flowers were arranged in. He handed Lily the card without comment.

Lily paused to thank the porter before tearing the envelope open. 'Who on earth?' Then she smiled, thinking, *Lara*.

Her twin had sent a daily text to ask after Emmy but they had not spoken at all. It had been their mother who had broken the news to Lara—the double news.

Watching her, Ben saw the smile and then saw it fall as she said, 'It's from your grandfather.'

'Who did you think it was from?'

Still frowning, she looked up from the card she had read twice now. 'What…? Oh, I thought it might be from Lara.'

It took him a few seconds to recognise the emotion that fell away when he realised the flowers weren't from an admirer—jealousy. Aware that Lily was looking expectantly at him, he pushed through the sense of shock and pulled himself together enough to respond. 'Of course, it would be.'

Ben had said little after he had told his grandfather, but it had gone a lot better than he'd anticipated.

'He says he's looking forward to meeting his great-granddaughter…' An old-fashioned sort of man, the elderly landowner was not the type of person who was relaxed about single parents. 'And he is happy to welcome me into the family…wow!' The sentiment was almost as over the top as the flowers.

'Aren't you surprised?' she persisted, talking to Ben's back as he stowed the flowers in the boot of the car before coming round to open the passenger door for her.

'Not really—he had about given up on me having children.'

'I really thought it would be awkward. I'm so relieved,' she admitted. 'I was worried that Mum might lose her home and job.'

Ben looked shocked by the suggestion. 'Good God, Lily, he's a stubborn old sod but he's not a monster. He'd never punish your mother for the sins of—'

'Me,' she completed, sliding into the car with a face set like a carved cameo to hold back the sudden desire to cry.

Cursing fluently, Ben went round to his side of the car and got in. The car purred into life and he turned to Lily.

'That wasn't what I was about to say. I was just mixing up my metaphors and if we are talking sin…fair enough, bring it on!'

The invitation brought her head around. Ben was looking straight ahead, but she sucked in a tiny breath as he turned to face her. The blaze of sheer hunger in his eyes sent a deep shudder from her scalp to her curling toes.

'Because I for one—' she froze, unable to move a muscle as his long, warm fingers curved around her jaw '—enjoyed it, very much.'

If her brain hadn't shut down she might have guessed what he meant to do, but it came as a total shock as, still holding her eyes, he fitted his mouth to hers.

Lily sighed, her eyes closing, her fingers clutching at air. The sensual caress deepened and her sigh became a soft moan in his mouth. He tasted so— Then it was over. His face stayed close to hers; she could feel his breath on her cheeks, on her eyelids.

'It felt like that, and it gave us Emily Rose. If you want to call it sin, fine. I call it something…rare, very rare.'

She felt his hand brush against her breast as he straightened away from her. The next moment the big car was moving with a low growl out of the illegal parking space.

'Damned roadworks!'

How did he do that? Her world had just shifted on its axis and he was acting as though nothing had happened between them. Layers of confusion on top of layers of fatigue meant that five minutes later she was wondering if any of that had actually just happened or had she fallen asleep and dreamt it all?

She was also wondering where she was. Lily held her tongue but as they turned into an affluent-looking tree-lined road of large private houses that overlooked a pretty park she had to say something. 'You're going the wrong way.'

'No, I'm going the right way.'

Lily sighed. What was it with men and admitting they were lost? 'I know I'm a mere woman but—' Her voice raised a panicky octave. 'Why are we stopping here?'

They had drawn up at the end of the road outside the last house. The largest by far, and Edwardian-looking, it was set back a long way and screened from the road by mature trees.

Presuming he was looking for some place to turn around, Lily twisted in her seat. As she did so the big high gates of the house opened and Ben drove through them. He brought the car to a halt on the cobbled fore-court.

He glanced at his phone. 'Fifteen minutes, not bad.'

'I suppose you're going to tell me what you're doing some time soon? Or am I meant to guess?' she asked crankily as she stifled a yawn. Weirdly the erotic incident felt as though it had happened to someone else.

'Didn't I say?' He held out a bunch of keys and dropped them in her lap. 'You're all set.' He swivelled in his seat and glanced up, a critical frown furrowing his brow at the well-kept period façade. 'So what do you think?'

'Of what? Look, Ben, I'm tired. I'm not really in the mood for a treasure hunt.' Or being kissed... *Liar, liar, pants on fire,* intoned the scornful voice in her head.

'It's not perfect,' he admitted, 'and clearly not a permanent solution, but there was not much choice within travelling distance of the hospital.' Before she could respond to this obscure comment, he had leapt athletically out of the car.

Pressing her fingers to her temples, she waited while he came around to open the passenger door.

'Have you got a headache?'

She dropped her hands, turned her head and looked at him. 'It's only a matter of time,' she predicted. 'Look, at this rate it will be time to get back to the hospital before I even get the B & B.' The fizz of adrenaline after the all-clear had got her this far, but Lily doubted it would get her much farther. Her head felt like cotton wool and even lifting an arm was an effort.

He nodded, his eyes skimming her pale features. 'You look totally spaced out,' he roughed out huskily.

Lily roused herself to respond tetchily, 'Well, you don't look like an oil painting either.'

If only that were true. Even barely able to keep her

eyelids open, just looking at him suffused her body with a deep ache of longing so intense that for a moment she couldn't breathe. No oil paint existed that could possibly begin to convey the level of sheer energy he exuded.

He lifted a rueful hand to the stubble on his jaw, his mobile lips quirked in grin. 'I'd like to think you love me for more than my body and sartorial elegance.'

She opened her mouth to retort in a similar style that she didn't love him at all when the light bulbs in her head started flashing. The blood drained from her face.

Love!

When…how did that happen?

Love…? Not the childish crush that had turned him into a hero figure or even the passionate primal response to him as a man, but a soul-deep longing.

'Not a perfect situation, obviously—'

She blinked. How long had she been sitting there with her mouth open? It had felt like a century, but Ben continued talking as if nothing had happened. Well, for him she supposed it hadn't.

'I picked up the keys this morning.'

She sat there trying to gather some strength before she levered herself out of the car with a gentle grunt of effort. There was no question of taking the hand he offered; she could barely look him in the face.

'You're staying here?' she said, struggling to move past this sudden paralysing shyness as she focused on the building behind him.

She liked its solid proportions and the magical little green oasis of its setting, but it seemed an odd choice for Ben, who she saw more as an industrial loft sort of man.

'Have you been listening to a word I've been saying?' His exasperation faded as he scanned her face. 'Come in,' he said, concern roughing his voice as he placed a guiding hand in the small of her back.

'I'm staying here?'

She walked ahead of him through the massive red door with its stained-glass panels. There were more panels in the big square hallway but, while most of the period features were in situ, including the mellow wood block floor, the décor was much more modern. The paintwork was all muted pastels, bright splashes of colour provided by an eclectic collection of modern art.

Feeling his eyes on her, she turned, looking at him through her lashes as she tipped her head. 'It's a very nice house,' she said politely.

'It's only temporary. I bought it fully furnished so—what do the estate agents always say, look past the décor? The previous owners used the cottage in the garden for the housekeeper...she could stay on.'

'I think it's lovely, but I don't really understand what it has got to do with me.' Her head was full of her discovery; houses came a very poor second to love. When had it happened? Was it normal for love to creep up this way? Had it been little things like the silly ties?

'I'll explain tomorrow. What you need now is sleep.' He glanced towards the big central staircase, wondering if she'd make it under her own steam.

Lily didn't move. 'You bought it...but why...?' And when did he have the time? 'Have you decided to move into property development?'

'Not at the moment. Look, by now we both know that they allow children home a lot quicker when they live close enough to make treatment or checks on a daily basis possible.'

'You bought a house so that Emmy could get home sooner...?' She choked back the emotional sob that was never far away, her voice quivering as she said quietly, 'You believed she'd get well.'

CHAPTER EIGHT

'I BELIEVED THAT you believed.'

Lily huffed out a tiny laugh, her lips twisting into a reflective, sad half-smile. 'I had to believe. The alternative... I couldn't have borne it.' She shook her head and looked around, wondering who would sell a home with all their possessions. 'I don't know what to say—you did all this? It's *too* much.'

He gave a shrug. Her gratitude made him uncomfortable. He might not have chosen to be an absent parent but the fact remained that she had been alone in bringing up his child and, though the past few weeks had not been normal, he was beginning to understand just how much of a responsibility that was. Or maybe that wasn't the discovery after all. It was a responsibility that he had been avoiding all his adult life. What he hadn't known then was the joy of seeing through a child's eyes, how something mundane could become a marvel.

'It's nothing.'

She gave a cracked laugh and did a three-sixty-degree turn that made her head spin. 'This is not nothing.'

He grabbed her arm to steady her. 'Compared to seeing Emmy smile, it is nothing.' His grandfather's words during that last argument came back to him.

'Your problem is you think it's all about profit, but it isn't. It's about people... You know the cost of everything and the value of nothing.'

Even though he'd mended bridges, Ben's jaw hardened at the memory, just as it had back then as he had watched his grandfather feed the proposal he had sweated over for months—the one that was to drag the estate into the twenty-first century—into the fire.

But maybe the old man had had a point. And if he'd not reacted to his hurt pride and instead of storming off had stayed and made him see that it wasn't all about the figures, there would have been no bridges to build. An image of his grandfather's lined face—it was the frailty that had shocked him—rose up, leaving a taste of regret in his mouth.

Clearing his throat, he didn't quite meet Lily's eyes as he shrugged his shoulders. 'We won't be out of pocket the way the market is. We could sell the place tomorrow and make money and it isn't totally altruistic—this is a big house.'

Her eyelashes fluttered as the comment sank in. She thought of the kiss and her insides quivered. Reading between the lines was an inexact science, especially when you were this exhausted. 'You plan to live here?'

He looked as if he was about to say something, then to her intense frustration shook his head decisively. 'Look, we can talk about this later. Right now what you need is sleep. I'll show you where the room is.'

She looked at the sweeping staircase and felt a surge of panic. 'You'll wake me if there is any news?'

'I promise.'

'And you won't let me sleep too long?'

In his view, a week would not be long enough for her, but he agreed.

He left her at the door of the room that was on the first floor, which was just as well because she was virtually asleep on her feet.

Lily barely registered the room as she headed for the bed, a modern limed-oak four-poster. With a sigh she closed her eyes and fell headlong onto it.

Bliss, she was asleep in seconds.

Coming to check on her fifteen minutes later, Ben tapped on the door that was still half open. When there was no reply he pushed it gently inwards; he could hear the sound of her soft breathing.

He crossed the room and, keeping one watchful eye on the sleeping figure, carefully lowered the Roman blinds on the window. The light dimmed but not significantly; the blinds were unlined. The heavy drapes would have provided a blackout, but, suspended by brass rings on a pole of the same material, would have made one hell of a racket so he left them alone.

As he passed the bed she sighed.

He had reached the door when he found himself walking back. He stood for a moment looking down at her. She lay on her stomach, one arm curved above her head, the other dangling over the edge of the bed. Her face half hidden by the pillow and her mane of glorious hair lightly flushed, she looked like a sleeping angel.

He unfolded a tartan throw that was neatly folded at the bottom of the bed and spread it carefully over her before easing off one calf-length boot and then the other.

'Marry her!' his grandfather had said, and of course, being the man he was, he had made it sound like an order, not a suggestion.

He had listened—not because the idea was anything less than ludicrous but because he knew that the old man, misguided and terminally old-fashioned as he was, had his best interests at heart.

'Compromise is not a dirty word. Life doesn't have to be a head-on collision.'

As he'd listened Ben had reluctantly acknowledged that his grandfather was not saying much he hadn't secretly thought himself.

He had not planned a family, but now he had one wouldn't it make sense to formalise things? The idea took hold and grew. He'd thought of it as a marriage of convenience because he'd been too much of a coward to face the truth. Today had changed that; he had been given a glimpse of what it would feel like to lose someone he loved.

How much worse would it feel to lose someone you loved and know you'd never had the guts to admit even to yourself that you loved her?

Not that anything was going to happen to Lily, his beautiful, marvellous Lily, not on his watch. He wanted to wake her up now and tell her; it took all his willpower not to.

There was no escaping the fact that his timing was disastrously out. Her focus was solely on Emily Rose and rightly so. Ben was pretty sure, considering he'd made no secret of the fact that he thought marriage was for mugs, that any proposal he made that included the word love would be treated with intense suspicion— she'd laugh him out of the room.

His jaw firmed as he turned and walked out of the room. He needed to think about the long game; he needed to prove that he could be the man she wanted, the man she needed. And not just in her bed—though that, he admitted to himself, was not such a bad place to start, though obviously not now when she was so emotionally vulnerable.

The house had a panelled study. Of all the rooms it showed the most sign of the removal of personal items. The bookshelves that lined one wall from floor to ceiling were empty except for a row of ancient encyclopaedias and a few dog-eared paperbacks. The wall over the heavy desk had several paler patches where paintings or maybe photos had been removed.

He opened his laptop on the desk and tried out the chair as a file popped onto his screen. For once it was a struggle to empty his head and focus, but in the end he managed an hour's work before he took a break. He must have dozed in the chair because the sun was no longer shining through the leaded French doors when he jolted awake with a start, the force of which made him surge out of his chair.

The high-pitched keening sound was nothing short of feral; it made the hairs on his neck stand on end. For a second he froze and then, as the second peal of screams rang out, he hit the ground running. Heart thudding, arms pumping, he flew up the stairs. The door hit the wall with a dull thud that made pictures on the opposite wall shudder.

The shadowed room was silent and empty but for the figure who was sitting bolt upright on the bed. Her eyes were wide and unfocused, staring straight ahead.

After all the nightmare images that had flickered

horror-movie style through his head, the relief to find her in one piece and not lying in a pool of blood or something equally dire made him feel light-headed.

He was across the room in seconds, kneeling on the bed beside her. He caught her arms; her skin was cool and damp with a layer of perspiration.

'What is it?' She looked at him with a total lack of recognition. He could feel the fine tremors running through her body. 'Lily, talk to me,' he roughed out huskily. 'What's wrong, baby?'

Her response was slow. A pucker appeared between her brows as she frowned at him and blinked like an owl.

'What's wrong, Lily? Say something.'

'I… I was asleep…was I…? Ben…what are you doing here?' And where was here? She felt slightly confused but not alarmed. His shirt was partly unbuttoned and his hair mussed as though he'd just tumbled out of bed, but he was still wearing jeans—Ben did things for denim that ought to carry a health warning. The erotic thought was only half formed when Lily stiffened. 'Emmy!'

Even before he had made suitably soothing noises and reassured her that Emmy was fine and would be fine, her brain had got there and the fear receded.

'You screamed.' He closed his eyes momentarily, trying to blank out the replay of the sound in his head; the surface of his skin was still raised with goose bumps.

She frowned. 'Did I?'

He stroked down her bare arms with his hands, pushing her gently back down. 'Go to sleep, angel. You were dreaming.'

Her nose wrinkled in confusion. 'I don't remember.'

He huffed out a laugh. He would not forget—the sound would stay with him for ever.

'That's all right, and normal with night terrors,' he was able to explain with confidence. It was years since he'd thought of the boy at school who used to have them regularly and he never remembered anything. He pressed a light kiss to her forehead, whispering softly, 'Go to sleep.'

Like a fairy-tale princess woken by a kiss, the fog cleared from her mind. Ben had begun to lever himself from the bed when she grabbed his arm.

He paused and covered the hand on his arm with his own. 'It's all right. You had a bad dream. Close your eyes. You're still asleep.'

She shook her head and, still holding his arm, her fingers digging hard into the muscles, she pulled herself upright again. Her eyes were burning, not with confusion, but a smouldering determination.

'You're not going to remember a thing about this tomorrow.'

Her green eyes wide and languid, she stroked his cheek, her fingers trailing slowly over the skin of his jaw. His jaw clenched as his self-control trembled, but stayed by some miracle intact.

'You're—'

She pressed a finger to his lips. 'I'm not asleep or sleepwalking. I'm totally lucid, see.' She directed a finger towards her own face. 'Awake.'

'I see,' he said thickly, looking into the beautiful heart-shaped face turned up to his. The dark shadows under her incredible eyes and her bare, natural face didn't alter the fact she was the most incredible-looking woman and he loved her.

* * *

'Stay, Ben,' she whispered urgently. 'Please, I don't want you to go. I don't want to be alone.'

He let out a long low groan; he could feel his self-control slipping through his fingers. 'You're killing me, Lily. I wish I could, I really do.' He brushed a tendril of hair from her face and found a spot of cold dampness on her cheek. 'You're crying,' he husked, framing her face between his big hands.

'Am I?'

She reached up and stroked his cheek. 'I want to be held.'

His blue eyes were almost black as their eyes locked. 'I wish I could.' A man had to know his limitations. And Ben had already gone beyond his. He wanted to comfort her but he knew that if he touched her he wouldn't stop there—he couldn't stop there.

'In the car you kissed me…'

He caught her hand and held it just away from his face.

Her long lashes fluttered downwards and then lifted as she said throatily, 'I liked it. Could you kiss me again?'

His glance slid to her full lips. Oh, he could kiss her again but it wouldn't stop there. *So what's so wrong with that?* asked the voice in his head.

She wanted, he wanted, they were both consenting adults, so what was holding him back? Precious little, came the answer. When she declared—

'Ben, *please*. I want you to make love to me!'

He had no control over his physical response but he could still have walked away; a better man would.

His eyes had darkened to navy; she could feel the

tension in his body as the muscle under her fingers tightened and bulged. Her stomach tensed, the muscles clamping in an anticipation that bordered on pain.

'Actually, I need you to make love to me.' After all the pretending, even to herself—especially to herself—it was a relief to say it. The depth of the emotions she was experiencing fed into her voice, making it husky as she rushed headlong into an explanation that fell short of actually explaining how she was feeling. 'I've been scared for so long. I just want to feel warm and safe and…' She paused. Even in the midst of her recklessness, she retained enough caution to conceal some things. 'Not alone,' she whispered. 'Do you know what I mean?'

He nodded slowly, the restraint he held himself under making his hand shake as his fingers touched her face. He intended to just brush her cheek, offering the safest version of the comfort she was asking for. Only once his fingers had made contact it was addictive, the texture of her skin, the thought of her warmth and softness, of sliding into it, into her, losing himself.

His fingers were framing one side of her face when his voice, made abrupt by the internal struggle, made a last-ditch effort to retain control. 'You're emotionally and physically whacked. You don't know what you're saying.'

She stared at him, disbelief mingling with the sting of utter mortification. 'Don't you dare tell me what I know and don't know!' she flung back furiously. 'And don't pretend you're being noble and chivalrous—just tell the truth. You don't fancy me? I can take it. I've been rejected by better men than you, you total bastard!'

He caught her hand before it connected with his

cheek and he dragged her backwards so that she ended
up sideways across the bed, lying full length on top of
him, her softness slotting into his angles as though they
were a designed fit. But there was nothing designed
about this. This was more a collision fuelled by raw
instinct and driving, aching need.

'I only deal in the possible and it is *not* possible that
any man has ever rejected you,' he slurred, his eyes following the line of her throat down to where her breasts
pressed against the cotton top she wore.

Lily, breathless, squirmed, managing to lever herself
into a sitting position astride him as she shrilled back,
'Let me go!' She felt him shudder and leaned in close
again to catch his low words.

'I'm not the one holding on.'

The fight drained out of her as she shook her head in
denial. The bonds of his hot, hungry stare were invisible but held her as firmly as steel chains.

Their eyes remained locked as the intense moment
stretched, filled with emotions too complex for her to
name. They formed in a deep knot of nameless yearn-
ing in her aching pelvis.

He flicked his wrists and caught hers, reversing the
role of captor and captured as he jerked her down hard.
Lily lost her grip on his shoulders and her elbows gave
way. With a soft cry she lay there, her breasts crushed
against him, her hair a flaming curtain that fell forward,
brushing his chest and face, their own shadowed silken
tent cutting out the outside world.

Holding her eyes, he tipped her over, bringing them
to lie side by side.

'You want this?'

She nodded and shivered as he slid his hand to her

breast, the breath hissing through her nostrils as she hitched in a sharp breath of pleasure and closed her eyes.

'I'm going to touch you.' His words trickled over her like warm honey.

'Where?' she whispered back.

He smiled and flicked his tongue across her earlobe. 'All over.'

'Truly?'

'Cross my heart.' He took her hand and placed it on his chest. Only a thin rim of green remained as her dilated pupils expanded some more.

'What will you do then?'

'I'll taste you.'

Her insides melted. 'I love looking at you.'

The confession drew a throaty growl as he hauled her hard up against him and fitted his mouth to hers. His lips moved with sensuous skill across her parted lips. By the time his tongue plunged deep she was floating on a sensual sea of pleasure and longing.

He kissed as though he'd drain her. She ought to have been feeling empty, but she felt more alive than she ever had in her life. As she kissed him back, winding her slim arms tight around his neck, she revelled in the feel of his male strength and his hard body.

The kiss was deepened, her small cry lost in his mouth as it went on and on. He was drinking her all and she wanted to just keep giving.

When they broke apart, both breathing hard, he looked as shaken as she felt.

'You sure?'

'Totally.'

The room was quiet as they undressed each other. There were many pauses along the way to touch and caress, to explore and admire, and when there were no longer clothes they lay down side by side on the bed.

His hand moved down her flank, drawing her leg across his hip as he cupped one perfect breast, stroking the tight, sensitised centre before he bent his head and fitted his mouth to it.

She sighed deeply and sank her fingers into his hair, stroking his scalp through the thick dark pelt. The drift of hair on his body was just as dark. He had a man's body. As he lifted his head she held his eyes while she ran a finger down the centre of his chest, following the thin dark demarcation line of his body hair over the flat belly and lower.

He groaned as she cupped him, curling her fingers around his erection before she slid slowly down his body, tracing the line her finger had made with her tongue.

He endured her ministrations for as long as he could until with a deep groan he grasped her shoulders. She lifted her head, her passion-filled eyes hot as she responded to his urging and slithered up along his body until they lay face to face, noses almost touching, sealed as close as bodies could get without penetration.

'My turn.'

'All over?'

There was a carnal intent in his slow smile as he tipped her onto her back and knelt over her. 'I never break a promise.'

He didn't. By the time he parted her legs and slid into her he had taken her to the edge several times, seeming to know exactly what she needed before she knew it herself, taking her places that she hadn't known were on the map!

When he finally entered her she was a screaming mess of pleasure-soaked nerve endings. The sensation of him moving inside her, beautifully filling her, driving her deeper into herself, making her aware of her own body, made the slow-burn fuse he had lit simply explode.

Coming back to earth was a gentle, warm feeling of contentment. She turned with a lazy smile to him. 'You really didn't miss anywhere. In fact you went places I didn't know I had.' Before pressing her face to his chest and falling asleep—no nightmares this time.

'What does a man have to do to wake up beside you in bed?' He made it sound like a joke, but it was deadly serious. When he'd woken at the crazily early hour to find nothing but the lingering perfume of her body in the space beside him, his sense of loss had been profound.

Lily picked up the freshly brewed pot of coffee, her expression staying composed as the sight of him standing there looking rumpled and utterly gorgeous with his feet bare, his jeans unbelted and his shirt open dismantled her nervous system cell by cell.

'I need to get back to the hospital.' She looked at the spoon in her hand and didn't have a clue how many spoonfuls of sugar she'd already put in so she thought, *What the hell?* And added another.

The horrible taste was something for her to focus on as he stepped further into the room wrapped in his aura of rampant sexuality.

'Last night,' she began, relieved that her words had halted his progress. If she aimed to keep the table between them, and of course didn't think about him throwing her on top of it and making love to her, it would be fine. Totally fine.

She had this worked out. There was no way she was going to lay herself open to the accusation of romanticising what had happened; she planned to get in there first.

He arched a brow and opened the fridge. 'I'm listening.'

'It was what I needed, so thank you.' She saw a look that was close to shock chase across his face—or was that relief? she wondered miserably. 'But I won't be requesting sympathy sex every night.' Request sounded a lot better than beg.

Ben, who had raised the carton of milk to his lips, had a choking fit. He turned, wiping a drip of milk off his chin.

'So is that what you think last night was?'

'Relax. I'm not going to start talking about deep and meaningful experiences.' Having him spell it out would have been too humiliating and embarrass them both. This way, even if he didn't believe her, she retained her dignity or what she had left of it—she had begged him! Disbelief mingled with toe-curling self-loathing. What had happened to her pride?

Still, at least she had managed to stop short of telling him she loved him, she reminded herself, focusing on the positive and how she could downplay it now.

'It was sex, pretty excellent sex—' She couldn't stop her eyes flying to his face as she added with a husky question mark, 'I think?' Lara wouldn't be asking, she'd be telling him; she'd be… *She* wasn't Lara.

He thought of the peace and sense of belonging he had found in her arms, in her body, and brought his lashes down in a concealing sweep. 'I think too.'

He put the carton back in the fridge and looked at her, his blue eyes still partially veiled by his crazy, gorgeous lashes as he lounged against the open stainless-steel door. 'Awkward, isn't it?'

Lily struggled to inject some sincerity into her smile, but as a person who had once reduced a drama-school teacher to tears with her interpretation of a tree she suspected she was doing a really pathetic job.

'Not at all, I'm fine. It's forgotten.'

Resisting the temptation to make her eat her lying words—or at least him—he closed the fridge with a bang that made her jump and turned back. 'If I did believe you, I'd be insulted,' he teased.

She missed the teasing note and her eyes widened in dismay. 'No, I didn't mean—you were marvellous!'

'Don't stop. It was just getting interesting.'

'That is, last night was…intense and with all the things going on I…that is…this is—'

'Awkward, like I said.' He passed a hand across his jaw, grimacing at the thick stubble. 'I suppose you rang the hospital already?'

She nodded. 'Everything's fine, but—'

'You want to get back. No problem, just give me five minutes to shower and you can think about my cure for the awkwardness.'

'What cure?'

He swung back. 'Oh, didn't I say? We should get

married. Think about it?' he said, as if he'd just asked her to decide if she wanted meringue or sticky toffee for her pudding.

CHAPTER NINE

LILY STOOD THERE for a full minute not thinking. Her brain barely breathing before she reacted, the time lapse meant he was in the bedroom they had shared the previous night before she reached him. Enough time for him to strip down to his boxers.

'For goodness' sake put some clothes on,' she said, struggling to keep her eyes above waist level. The boxers left very little to the imagination and hers had already gone into overdrive.

'I don't shower dressed.'

'And I don't appreciate your sense of humour,' she countered resentfully. 'What the hell was that down there?'

His grin flashed and he dropped his gaze down his own body. 'I'm insulted you have to ask. I kind of thought it was pretty obvious.'

Her face burned as she dragged her eyes to face level. *It was.* 'I meant downstairs…in the kitchen.'

'A proposal of marriage?'

'It would serve you right if I said yes,' she hissed back, spitefully thinking, *Lara got a man who stopped a plane to propose to her and I…I get a joke?* She bit down on her quivering lip and thought, *I don't want dramatic gestures. I want one little word—love.*

'I hope you do, Lily.'

She stared, her eyes widening as she searched his face for any sign of deceit. 'You're not serious!' But she could see he was and she felt scared, excited and appalled all at the same time. 'Why?'

There was only one answer that, to her mind, was a reason for contemplating marriage—it wasn't the one he gave.

'I don't want my daughter to be brought up by another man.' *Keep the woman you love close and the woman you want to convince you love her closer...* He thought in all modesty that it worked better than the original he had shamelessly borrowed from.

This comment reduced her excitement levels and brought her crashing down to earth with a bang. 'You've nothing to prove to me, Ben.' She thought she was concealing her terrible disappointment pretty well. 'You're a good father.'

His brows knitted as he struggled to follow her line of argument and understand the odd flatness in her voice. 'I'm not trying to prove anything.'

She pasted on a smile. 'We've gone way beyond that. The last few weeks you've been a rock.'

He gritted his teeth over his frustration at her response. 'I don't want to be a *rock*. I want to be your husband.'

'No,' she contradicted. 'You *want* to be Emmy's dad, you *want* to do the right thing and please your grandfather.' *Say you love me... I'd take a lie, just say it please!*

'What the hell has my grandfather got to do with it?'

'Are you trying to tell me he doesn't want you to make an honest woman of me? Tell him you asked and

I said no—he can't blame you for that. Marriage is tough even when people love one another,' she said, thinking of her twin again, this time not with envy as Lara's marriage was going through a bad…maybe terminal patch. 'Without it…?'

She gave another shrug, wondering if his silence meant he was secretly relieved that she had refused. Not that he was showing it—he still seemed pretty tense.

'I'm *glad* you're in Emmy's life and no matter who I might meet in the future that will not affect your relationship with Emmy. It's a sweet idea, but no.'

'Sweet…?' he echoed, thinking that he would dismember any man who so much as looked at her.

She nodded. 'Insane, but sweet,' she said sadly.

'What about last night?'

She felt her tight control slip a notch and increased the voltage of her smile to compensate. 'Last night was… We've both been living with a lot of stress lately.'

Ironically, if she hadn't been so passionately in love with him she might have considered his proposal, but feeling the way she did it was impossible. A non-starter. She couldn't settle for less…she couldn't live a lie… It would be like dying a little more each day.

'Look, I know I've kind of sprung this on you but after last night there didn't seem any point waiting.'

Because I'm gagging for it, she thought, keeping her lips firmly clamped over the humiliating thought.

'All I'm asking is you keep an open mind. The fact is we find ourselves doing things we didn't think we would all the time. I never thought I'd be a father but I am and it's one of the best things that has ever happened to me.'

Her anger slipped away as his simple sincerity brought a lump to her throat. 'And you're really great at it, and I realise that this is because of Emmy, you think that this is right for her but—'

'Let me be honest.'

Lily could count the number of times on one hand that those words were followed by something that made her feel good—it turned out this time was no exception.

'I felt as you do, that marriage as a piece of paper was irrelevant.'

Lily stared at him, astonished. Was that what he had heard her say?

'You were engaged to be married when you slept with me the first time.'

His brows lifted as he struggled to decide if the jealousy he detected in her voice was wishful thinking or actually there. 'I really wasn't.'

'How would *she* feel if you get married?'

'Caro!' he exclaimed, looking astonished. 'What the hell has it got to do with her?'

Lily lowered her lashes. 'You're still best friends.'

He threw back his head and laughed. 'Who says?'

Lily's chin lifted. 'She does, in the dedication of her new bestseller.'

One of the nurses on the ward had come on duty with a signed copy that she had shown around. The photo on the fly leaf, according to her, did not do the blonde cookery writer justice.

'That was her idea of a joke. Caro and I were once an item. We were *not* engaged. That was just a publicity stunt—she was launching a new career. As for best friends, Caro and I have not been in contact since we split up, though she did send me a copy of her new book.

She really is a great cook. If we'd got married I'd be the size of a tank by now.'

He glanced down and patted his muscle-toned belly. Lily stared at it too, struggling to imagine a blurring of the lines of his hard, lean body and failing.

'She is history. I am a man with a family—I want to be a man with a family. *So?*'

'You don't have to marry me to be a family. Emmy is your family.'

Ben fought the impulse to drag her into his arms and kiss her into submission. 'I don't want to be a weekend father.'

'You can see Emmy whenever you want,' she said, feeling like a hypocrite as she thought, *It means I can see you.*

'Do you really want to share out the important events in our daughter's life—you get Christmas, I get Easter?' He saw her expression and drove his point home.

'I don't know, Ben—' *Couldn't he see she wanted love, not practicality?*

He cut across her, sensing a weakening of her resolve.

'That's what trial runs are for—turning the *don't knows* into *do knows*.'

I do know I love you, she thought bleakly.

'Look, when Emily Rose is home you'll be here— whether I have sleepover rights or I cook the breakfast is your call totally. But look at it this way—what have you got to lose?' *I have everything to lose,* he thought, smiling as he waited, every nerve fibre in his body tense for her reply.

She'd seen him every day for weeks—what if that

stopped? It was the idea of going cold turkey rather than his compelling argument that made her waver.

'I suppose it could work...but not... We share the house, but not the bedroom.'

The conversation came to a halt; a nerve clenched and unclenched in his cheek. 'And what is that meant to prove?'

'You said you'd cook breakfast and it was my decision.'

'It is.' It was just not the one he'd wanted or expected to hear.

'I want more.'

He began to walk towards her with a slow, deliberate tread, a gleam in his eyes. 'I can give you more.'

The leashed power in him made her senses spin. 'I know you can, but...' She backed away, hand up in a defensive gesture, but as the things she was defending herself against were all inside her the gesture was pretty useless.

'But what?' When she said nothing he added, 'Marry me.'

Biting her lip, Lily felt her determination waver just as he added, 'For Emmy.' As if it were the winning argument, not knowing ironically that it was what gave her the strength to shake her head.

If she was to survive loving Ben and having him in her life for Emmy's sake, Lily knew she had to distance herself, emotionally and physically—the two were interlinked. 'I just don't think you've thought this through.'

He dragged a hand through his hair, leaving it spiked as he sat back on the bed. 'I've thought about little else!'

'I know you love Emmy and you've planned all this.'

Her gesture encompassed the room and beyond. 'You want to make up for lost time. But I don't want to play at happy families. Ben, when I get married I want it to be for the right reasons.'

'Last night felt pretty right to me.'

'That was sex. We can share the parenting. This is a big house...'

He turned his head slowly. 'You think we can share this house and not a bed?'

'We can be civilised...'

He rose to his feet and towered over her not looking at all civilised, looking primitive and raw. She struggled to catch her breath—he was awesome.

'Speak for yourself,' he growled. His expression toughened as he came to a decision. 'The only promise I'm making is I won't knock on your door in the middle of the night.'

'You think I will?' she exclaimed. 'You think I'm that desperate?'

He gave a slow smile. 'Oh, yeah, quite definitely.'

Her chin went up. 'I'm not that person.' *Oh, yes,* said the voice in her head, *you are, Lily. You really are.*

Lily was going to have a chance to find out sooner than she had anticipated. It was two days later that Emmy's discharge was agreed.

The discharge papers were signed, the outpatient appointment booked, but there was a last-minute rush when the medication Emmy needed had not come up from the pharmacy.

Lily was in the middle of packing when the nurse who had been sent for them appeared.

'Sorry about the delay, but I've got them now.'

'Don't worry, I still haven't finished packing. I've no idea how we accumulated this much stuff in a few weeks,' Lily huffed, trying to stuff Emmy's favourite blanket into the open bag while she balanced her daughter on one hip, a task made more difficult by the tingle on the back of her neck that told her Ben was back in the room.

He handled delays, or anything that smacked in his opinion of incompetence, badly, so in the end she'd begged him to go walk it off because him glowering was not helping.

'Here, let me help you.' The nurse took Emmy and handed her to Ben, saying, 'Dad can hold her.'

Lily straightened up in time to see her daughter pull her father's lip, twisting the skin experimentally between her small fingers.

'Emmy, that hurts!' Lily knew from experience that it did.

'Aww, kiss Dada better...' cooed the nurse.

The baby landed a damp smack on Ben's cheek and giggled. 'Dada, Dada...'

Above their daughter's head she met Ben's eyes. The emotion she saw there made her throat close over until she closed her eyes and felt a tear squeeze out. Damn, she had spent the last two days building her walls and one look and they were gone.

Share a house? He was right: it was insanity!

Two weeks later Lily had changed her mind. The only insane thing here was her. It had been building up, but the actual crisis point came as she was sniffing a sweater that Ben had left slung untidily on a chair.

'What are you doing?' she asked herself.

She could have the man and she was sniffing his clothing like some sort of…addict! If this went on she would go insane; it was killing her!

And Ben knew it, she thought darkly. Oh, he hadn't said anything, but she knew he did. She did not think for one minute that there was any real need for him to walk around the house half naked and brush against her the way he did. He was torturing her and… She pressed a hand to her heaving chest and closed her eyes. God, but she ached with love for him.

She sank weakly into a chair. This had been totally unrealistic, a crazy idea… Share a house…? What had she been thinking?

She hadn't; she should have told him the truth. Oh, yes, and that would have worked—*I can't marry you, Ben, because I love you, and I know you won't ever feel the same about me.*

She gave a laugh and then stopped. Was it a joke? She was so emotionally worn down by this point, she was such a mass of hormonal craving and blind lust that once she started talking it would all come out.

And why not? she thought recklessly. Why not be honest and come clean?

Would her honesty have a price?

It didn't matter because being around him every day and being forced to conceal her feelings was a form of slow death and anyway didn't he *deserve* to know the truth?

He had asked her to marry him—didn't he have the right to know *why* she had refused? And had she been right? Was she selfish wanting more? Emmy loved him; he was a great father.

Her thoughts went round in dizzying circles, until

the doorbell rang. Lily leapt to her feet. Someone had their hand on the bell and she knew from bitter experience that if Emmy woke early from her nap she would be cranky all afternoon.

'Idiot,' she muttered before calling, 'I'm coming!'

A total waste!

His morning had been a total waste.

He had come very close to cancelling.

There had been several points during the excruciatingly polite conversation over breakfast when she had not even looked him in the eyes and he had been *this* far from snapping.

There was a certain black irony to the situation. All his life his focus had been on maintaining a safe distance from emotional entanglements; he'd seen marriage as a trap.

He'd called it common sense but it had been fear. The irony being that he was frequently referred to as fearless, a risk taker, but, when it came to the things that were important in life, Ben recognised he had been nothing but a coward.

Now the woman who had taught him that he was not only capable of love but that he *needed* love was keeping an emotional mile between them!

Hell, he'd had some low spots in his life but he'd never woken up every morning feeling so dark and desolate. Everything he wanted was there within arm's reach, but it might as well be a million miles away. He could let it continue—not an option—or he could actually *do* something about it—better late than never.

And she wasn't happy; he knew that. He couldn't *make* her love him, but he could damn well try and he would.

His thought solidified into purpose as middle-aged bankers, who between them could alter world money markets, continued to act like star-struck teenagers. He almost expected them to ask for autographs when the Hollywood couple at the next table came over to say goodbye to him. They'd slipped out of the rear entrance of the hotel to avoid the paparazzi pack who had been joined by three film crews out front.

Such was the power of celebrity, but on the plus side at least he'd managed to secure some hefty donations from them when he'd explained the couple supported a charity he championed.

He even managed to maintain this philosophical attitude when counting the minutes until he could get back home. He stepped out onto the street and was hit with a battery of flashes, which quickly abated when they realised he was not even half of their quarry, though obviously it was flattering to be mistaken for the man that had been dubbed the sexiest man in the universe.

As the cameras were lowered someone recognised him and called out his name, another took up the call and the flashes began again. *So near but so far,* he thought as he saw his limo pull into the kerb.

Ben had made a conscious decision early on not to court the media. It was about balance. They were a presence in his life that was unavoidable. His face made a few society pages and the financial papers liked to quote him but he seriously doubted he could live with the level of media intrusion enjoyed—or not—by the couple who had escaped the pack.

If he was seen falling out of nightclubs or frequenting pole-dancing establishments, he had no doubt he

would have had his own pack of press stalkers, but he
didn't. His name rarely made it to the tabloids and it
was hard to imagine what story they could spin from
his breakfast meeting, but everyone, he thought, school-
ing his features into impassivity, had to make a living.

Frustrated by his indifference and lack of response,
a few tried to goad him into responding by throwing
out a few suggestions for him to deny.

Ben ignored them and the cameras being thrust in
his face. The doorman, who had walked ahead of him,
opened his limo door; he was literally a couple of feet
away when it happened.

Every head including Ben's turned towards the tall
gorgeous redhead poured into a clashing bright neon-
pink minidress that hugged her sinuous curves. The
press pack parted like the Red Sea for her as she ran
towards Ben like a heat-seeking missile in five-inch
heels.

Oh, hell! For some reason Lily's twin was about to
present the press pack with a photo opportunity and
he had no way to stop it, short of rugby tackling her or
trying out a useful judo move.

In the event it seemed unlikely that either would have
stopped the woman, who was extremely determined.
She oozed all over him, plastering herself against him
like a second skin. As she lifted her face and gave a
predatory smile he got a face full of alcohol fumes—
definitely wasted! Light a match and they'd have gone
up in flames!

He stood rigid as she wound her arms around his
neck. Her fingers dug into his scalp as she jerked his
head down and she went in for the kiss.

The entire sordid thing was a headline writer's wet

dream, he thought as he finally managed to bundle her into the waiting car!

'Just drive!'

His passenger had begun to gently snore.

CHAPTER TEN

As SHE RAN into the hall the bell got louder but to Lily's relief there were no cries from upstairs, and she'd have heard because since Ben had had the nursery wired for sound the sophisticated monitor system meant she could hear a pin drop in the nursery from anywhere in the house. It meant she was no longer running up the stairs at every imagined sound of distress.

'I'm coming!'

A scowl on her face, she flung open the door and stood there as her chin hit her chest.

'Thank God!'

Lily wasn't thanking God, she was feeling slightly queasy as she stood to one side to allow Ben with her twin slung over his shoulder entry into the hall. Like a clockwork automaton, she turned and closed the door behind her.

'This,' he said, turning to face her, 'is not what it looks like.'

'Lil…Lil…' The slurred voice trailed away as the redhead flopped down again.

'She just appeared out of nowhere… She's not sober.'

'I can smell that.' The initial stab of sheer visceral jealousy had receded, but the sight of Ben with her twin, wearing a dress that was a wardrobe malfunction waiting to happen, slung over his shoulder remained an image that did not fill her with joy.

'I didn't have a clue what to do with her so…'

'You brought her home.'

'Not really a plan, more…desperation,' he admitted and took a deep breath. 'I should probably tell you— your sister kissed me, and it was filmed.'

'Did you enjoy it?'

He shuddered. 'I did not!'

'Hey! I'm a very, *verrry* good kisser.' The slurs returned to snores.

Ben rolled his eyes, his mouth twisting in a moue of distaste. 'She's totally off her head.'

'You did the right thing,' Lily said nobly as her sister lifted her head and slurred again.

'Congratulations…can I be best man…no, maid of honour…?' Her head dropped and a moment later there was another gentle but audible snore.

'Do you suppose she needs a doctor?' Lily asked worriedly.

'What she needs is to sleep it off.'

Lily nodded towards the stairs. 'I expect you're right.'

She walked behind him as he carried Lara up the stairs, opening the door of the nearest guest bedroom when they reached the top.

Without hesitation Ben dropped his burden on the bed and heaved a relieved sigh. 'Can you cope from here? I've had enough of your sister for one day.'

Lily nodded.

It took her half an hour to settle Lara safely. When she went back downstairs Ben was nursing a whisky.

'I know it's only twelve o'clock but I need it. Your sister is...' He shuddered. 'God, she's a total nightmare!'

His obvious disgust made it easier to be generous and, anyway, Lily was genuinely worried about her twin. 'Not really, she's... I think she's just very unhappy. There are things going on...marriage problems.' Lily's compassionate heart ached for her twin. She had no doubt that she would get the full story once Lara sobered up.

Ben was less sympathetic. 'I'm not surprised! You'd need to be a saint to be married to her. The woman is unbalanced. I have no idea what her problem is and quite frankly I don't want to.'

'Do you think I should sit with her in case she wakes—?'

'No, I do not.' He put down his glass and moved closer, his gaze trained on her face. 'Were you jealous?'

'A little. She was always... I always felt invisible when Lara was around.'

'Sibling rivalry?'

'No. I didn't compete. Lara was always better at everything.'

He reached out and touched her face, husking, 'You're worth a hundred of the Laras of this world.'

She smiled. 'I was jealous for a second,' she admitted. 'When I saw you holding her. But then I saw your face.' A small bubble of laughter escaped her lips.

'Glad someone thinks it's funny.'

A worried expression replaced Lily's smile as she admitted, 'I'm pretty sure her husband might not see the joke...' From what she had seen of the man he was not the non-jealous type. 'We could always tell people it was me?'

Ben shot her brilliant plan down in flames. 'We will not.'

'But what if Raoul comes here thinking—?'

'I can look after myself,' he interrupted, sounding amused.

'And me...you have me, Ben. Me and Emmy. This has been and always will be a special time for me.' Her voice thickened with emotion as she gulped. 'I have some lovely memories, ones that I will treasure, but I can't carry on stringing you along like this. You deserve more,' she told him, tears standing out in her eyes as she looked up at him.

Ben stood there like a statue carved from stone, all expression wiped from his face. Had he left it too late?

'You deserve the truth, the reason why I can't marry you, why I never will.'

He moved then, lurching forward, his face locked in a grimace of anguish. 'Is there someone else? That doctor...?' His eyes narrowed as he recalled the young medic who had been sniffing around, being far too attentive.

'What? No, of course not, there's no one.' The tears threatened again. 'There never will be anyone. No!' She took a step backwards to evade him, knowing full well that if he touched her her resolve would dissolve.

'I can't marry you because I love you.'

She waited but his expression gave little clue as to what he was thinking or even if he believed her.

'Sorry, but you can see now that the marriage of convenience thing won't work for me.'

'Fine.'

Lily swallowed. She had hoped he'd take it well, but not *this* well!

She turned, struggling to match his casual manner. It wasn't as if she enjoyed dramatic scenes or anything. 'I should ring Mum to let her know Lara is all right. She rang last night to say she'd had an odd call from her.'

'No.'

'What?'

'Not now.' He grabbed her arm and swung her towards him. 'Say it again.'

She shook her head. 'Say what?' Their eyes connected and the eloquent glow she saw in his made her suck in a taut gasp. 'We've drifted apart over the last few years—'

'We have drifted *together* over the last few weeks.'

'I'm not talking about us, I'm talking about Lara and me.'

He swore under his breath. 'I don't want to talk about Lara.'

'What do you want?'

'I want to hear you say it again, the reason why you can't marry me.'

'I love you.' She lifted her chin; she'd thrown her pride away and it no longer mattered.

'There's no chance this is something temporary?'

She shook her head unhappily.

'You didn't want it to happen, but it did?'

Her eyes fluttered wide. 'How do you know that?'

'Because it happened to me too. I always thought I wasn't capable of loving anyone…and I was glad of it. I was an idiot but you taught me, Lily, you taught me what love is… You made me whole. I love you, Lily, with all my heart.'

The simple sincerity of his words, the emotional throb in his deep voice, made her eyes fill with tears of joy. She shook her head, still unable to quite believe this was happening. 'Why didn't you tell me, Ben? I've been so miserable, pretending.'

'I was waiting...'

'For what?'

'I wanted to prove to you that I was genuine, that I was worthy of you, committed.'

'You made me think that all you cared about was being a father to Emmy.'

'I was trying not to rush you...' A shade of indignation slid into his voice. 'How the hell was I to know you loved me?' Before she could respond he bent his head, putting all the pent-up frustration of the last two weeks in the deep, hard, penetrating kiss.

She surfaced with a dreamy smile. 'If you'd done that I might have told you,' she admitted.

'I had this plan in my head. I wanted to get everything right. I had this idea that the work at Warren Court would be finished, though obviously if I'd known you loved me I'd have thrown the plan out the window.'

She tugged at his shirt to get his attention and received more of it than she had anticipated as he claimed her mouth again in a series of hard, hungry kisses that merged into one and left her feeling drained and incredibly happy.

'Work on Warren...?' she mumbled against his mouth.

'Yes, this place is a bit small and my grandfather is getting too old to live there alone. We thought that a ground-floor apartment would give him privacy—'

'We? A conspiracy...?' Before he could respond to the teasing she pressed her hand to his mouth. 'What is this with you and houses? I don't give that—' she clicked her fingers with an expressive snap '—about houses. It's people that I care about, you and Emmy. I love you so much, Ben—'

The rest was lost in his mouth as he kissed her until her head spun. When he placed her back on her feet she needed his support to stop her falling over.

She might have said he had kissed her senseless, but actually she realised she had only just come to her senses.

He stroked her face with a loving hand. 'I don't care about where I live either. My home is anywhere you are. I just wanted to prove to you that I was sincere, that I could be a good father and husband, that I am totally into this.'

Heart singing with joy she had never imagined ever feeling, she slipped her arms around his waist, tilted her head back to look up into his face. 'Are you totally into me too?'

His mouth curved into a wicked grin. 'Oh, absolutely—and ready and willing to prove it.'

'Can you get upstairs without buying another house?'

'I'll try,' he promised, scooping her up. At the door, he paused. 'I should say there is a builder stopping by tomorrow. I thought I'd do a few renovations before I hand it over to the hospital… With a bit of work it could be perfect for families who find themselves in the situation we did.'

Lily's eyes filled with tears. 'Oh, Ben, that's a lovely idea.'

'I just hope that some of them have the happy ending we have had. This time last year my life was empty, and now I have…everything I need.'

Lily framed his face with her hands. 'So do I.' Adding, 'Shush,' as he ran up the stairs with her. 'We don't want to wake Lara. Too late,' she added as there was the sound of someone loudly weeping from the door they were passing. 'Sorry, Ben...'

He sighed. 'Well, just remember where we were and promise me that if she comes to our wedding you'll hide the booze.'

'You wanted family life,' she teased.

He covered the hand she had placed on the door handle with his and looked down with fierce longing into her face. 'I've always wanted you. I always will.'

A few weeks later they exchanged vows in front of their friends and relations, but for Lily what he said at that moment meant so much more.

EPILOGUE

Emily Rose Warrender
Year One Homework.
MY WEEKEND.

I was going to ride my pony this weekend. He's cool, but my mummy and daddy had to go to the hospital, so I stayed with my grandma and we played tea parties because she is quite old, maybe even twenty, and she needs to sit down a lot.

Mummy and Daddy brought home a baby this morning. Mummy says he looks like Daddy, but I don't think so because my daddy is very tall and handsome and baby Harry is wrinkled and red. My mummy has red hair like me and she is very pretty and so am I.

Harry can't do anything yet but Daddy says when he's older, maybe next week, I can teach him stuff like how to kick a ball and other things that I'm very good at. Daddy says I can be the boss.

I love my mummy and daddy a lot, and Harry, but my pony is better. I am going to be a very good boss.

* * * * *

MILLS & BOON®
Hardback – September 2015

ROMANCE

The Greek Commands His Mistress	Lynne Graham
A Pawn in the Playboy's Game	Cathy Williams
Bound to the Warrior King	Maisey Yates
Her Nine Month Confession	Kim Lawrence
Traded to the Desert Sheikh	Caitlin Crews
A Bride Worth Millions	Chantelle Shaw
Vows of Revenge	Dani Collins
From One Night to Wife	Rachael Thomas
Reunited by a Baby Secret	Michelle Douglas
A Wedding for the Greek Tycoon	Rebecca Winters
Beauty & Her Billionaire Boss	Barbara Wallace
Newborn on Her Doorstep	Ellie Darkins
Falling at the Surgeon's Feet	Lucy Ryder
One Night in New York	Amy Ruttan
Daredevil, Doctor...Husband?	Alison Roberts
The Doctor She'd Never Forget	Annie Claydon
Reunited...in Paris!	Sue MacKay
French Fling to Forever	Karin Baine
Claimed	Tracy Wolff
Maid for a Magnate	Jules Bennett

MILLS & BOON®
Large Print – September 2015

ROMANCE

The Sheikh's Secret Babies	Lynne Graham
The Sins of Sebastian Rey-Defoe	Kim Lawrence
At Her Boss's Pleasure	Cathy Williams
Captive of Kadar	Trish Morey
The Marakaios Marriage	Kate Hewitt
Craving Her Enemy's Touch	Rachael Thomas
The Greek's Pregnant Bride	Michelle Smart
The Pregnancy Secret	Cara Colter
A Bride for the Runaway Groom	Scarlet Wilson
The Wedding Planner and the CEO	Alison Roberts
Bound by a Baby Bump	Ellie Darkins

HISTORICAL

A Lady for Lord Randall	Sarah Mallory
The Husband Season	Mary Nichols
The Rake to Reveal Her	Julia Justiss
A Dance with Danger	Jeannie Lin
Lucy Lane and the Lieutenant	Helen Dickson

MEDICAL

Baby Twins to Bind Them	Carol Marinelli
The Firefighter to Heal Her Heart	Annie O'Neil
Tortured by Her Touch	Dianne Drake
It Happened in Vegas	Amy Ruttan
The Family She Needs	Sue MacKay
A Father for Poppy	Abigail Gordon

MILLS & BOON®
Hardback – October 2015

ROMANCE

Claimed for Makarov's Baby	Sharon Kendrick
An Heir Fit for a King	Abby Green
The Wedding Night Debt	Cathy Williams
Seducing His Enemy's Daughter	Annie West
Reunited for the Billionaire's Legacy	Jennifer Hayward
Hidden in the Sheikh's Harem	Michelle Conder
Resisting the Sicilian Playboy	Amanda Cinelli
The Return of Antonides	Anne McAllister
Soldier, Hero...Husband?	Cara Colter
Falling for Mr December	Kate Hardy
The Baby Who Saved Christmas	Alison Roberts
A Proposal Worth Millions	Sophie Pembroke
The Baby of Their Dreams	Carol Marinelli
Falling for Her Reluctant Sheikh	Amalie Berlin
Hot-Shot Doc, Secret Dad	Lynne Marshall
Father for Her Newborn Baby	Lynne Marshall
His Little Christmas Miracle	Emily Forbes
Safe in the Surgeon's Arms	Molly Evans
Pursued	Tracy Wolff
A Royal Temptation	Charlene Sands

0915 GEN STD HB

MILLS & BOON®
Large Print – October 2015

ROMANCE

The Bride Fonseca Needs	Abby Green
Sheikh's Forbidden Conquest	Chantelle Shaw
Protecting the Desert Heir	Caitlin Crews
Seduced into the Greek's World	Dani Collins
Tempted by Her Billionaire Boss	Jennifer Hayward
Married for the Prince's Convenience	Maya Blake
The Sicilian's Surprise Wife	Tara Pammi
His Unexpected Baby Bombshell	Soraya Lane
Falling for the Bridesmaid	Sophie Pembroke
A Millionaire for Cinderella	Barbara Wallace
From Paradise...to Pregnant!	Kandy Shepherd

HISTORICAL

A Mistress for Major Bartlett	Annie Burrows
The Chaperon's Seduction	Sarah Mallory
Rake Most Likely to Rebel	Bronwyn Scott
Whispers at Court	Blythe Gifford
Summer of the Viking	Michelle Styles

MEDICAL

Just One Night?	Carol Marinelli
Meant-To-Be Family	Marion Lennox
The Soldier She Could Never Forget	Tina Beckett
The Doctor's Redemption	Susan Carlisle
Wanted: Parents for a Baby!	Laura Iding
His Perfect Bride?	Louisa Heaton

MILLS & BOON®

Why shop at millsandboon.co.uk?

Each year, thousands of romance readers find their perfect read at millsandboon.co.uk. That's because we're passionate about bringing you the very best romantic fiction. Here are some of the advantages of shopping at www.millsandboon.co.uk:

* **Get new books first**—you'll be able to buy your favourite books one month before they hit the shops

* **Get exclusive discounts**—you'll also be able to buy our specially created monthly collections, with up to 50% off the RRP

* **Find your favourite authors**—latest news, interviews and new releases for all your favourite authors and series on our website, plus ideas for what to try next

* **Join in**—once you've bought your favourite books, don't forget to register with us to rate, review and join in the discussions

Visit **www.millsandboon.co.uk**
for all this and more today!